# Lawman's Choice

# LAWMAN'S CHOICE

## RAY HOGAN

**THORNDIKE**
**CHIVERS**

This Large Print edition is published by Thorndike Press, Waterville, Maine USA and by BBC Audiobooks Ltd, Bath, England.

Thorndike Press is an imprint of Thomson Gale, a part of The Thomson Corporation.

Thorndike is a trademark and used herein under license.

The text of this Large Print edition is unabridged.
Other aspects of the book may vary from the original edition.
Set in 16 pt. Plantin.

**LIBRARY OF CONGRESS CATALOGING-IN-PUBLICATION DATA**

Hogan, Ray, 1908–
    Lawman's choice / by Ray Hogan.
      p. cm. — (Thorndike Press large print Western)
    ISBN 0-7862-9132-X (alk. paper)
    1. Large type books. I. Title.
    PS3558.O3473L3 2006
    813'.54—dc22                        2006028981

BRITISH LIBRARY CATALOGUING-IN-PUBLICATION DATA AVAILABLE

Published in 2006 in the U.S. by arrangement with
Golden West Literary Agency.
Published in 2007 in the U.K. by arrangement with Golden West Literary Agency.

U.S. Hardcover: ISBN 13: 978-0-7862-9132-8; ISBN 10: 0-7862-9132-X
U.K. Hardcover: 978 1 405 63990 3 (Chivers Large Print)
U.K. Softcover: 978 1 405 63991 0 (Camden Large Print)

Printed in the United States of America on permanent paper
10 9 8 7 6 5 4 3 2 1

for . . .
Whitney Erin Hogan

# 1

They wouldn't be waiting for him, Matt Kollister thought, as he studied the dozen or so persons gathered in the dusty street ahead of him.

The town's name, he'd noted a bit earlier, was Shoham, and from where he had now halted on a narrow bridge that spanned a briskly flowing creek, it appeared to be a fairly large settlement as settlements went in that part of Texas — or was he in New Mexico?

From a habit recently intensified, Matt twisted about on the bay gelding he was riding and threw a glance along his back trail. Larkin was not in sight. That was good. He'd seen no sign of the lawman since late the previous day, and Matt reckoned he had finally shaken him. But that would only be temporary; he knew Fred Larkin well enough to realize the old marshal would never give up, that he would keep on search-

7

ing until he had found his quarry. However, if all went right as Matt planned, Larkin would be too late. Mexico, and sanctuary from American law, were now little more than a day's ride away — if that.

Kollister smiled bitterly. Lawman chasing lawman! That was a hell of a note. And, what was even worse, it was friend pursuing friend. He and Larkin had known each other for years — ten at least — ever since he'd hired on as a deputy in the county where Fred was serving as sheriff. Larkin had been like a father to him, teaching him about the law and the ways of men, and it had been Fred who'd recommended Matt for town marshal of Tiuga, a settlement in western Colorado, when the opportunity arose.

Tiuga . . . A hardness filled Kollister's wide-set gray eyes, turning them to colorless agates as he fell into deep thought. Tall and muscular, he had a square-cut face that wore two weeks' growth of beard, and his ordinarily trim mustache was ragged and in need of attention. The black, flat-crowned hat covering his head was streaked and stained by sweat and dust; his shirt and cord pants, the legs of which were thrust into badly scarred boots, also attested to the rigors of many days and nights on the run.

Despite his worn, almost beggarly appearance, there was the look of invulnerability to the man that bespoke strength and character and a belief in his abilities to cope with any situation — yet inwardly Matt Kollister was suffering deeply. Wounded not by bullets but by the actions of friends for whom he cared, had even risked his life, he had known disillusionment when they had turned from him the one time he had needed them.

He supposed he could have done something about that, perhaps gone to them, begged for their support, but it was not in him to do that. Pride in himself, in what he was and what the star he wore at the time represented, would not permit it. He had simply stated his position truthfully and accurately in the matter in question — a charge of murder — and relied on those he knew to back him.

It was at the point when those same persons had failed him that he had said to hell with it — to hell with friends and justice and the law and the whole damn thing. He'd been a lawman all of his adult life, and it had earned him nothing but endless days and nights of hard, dangerous toil — at the end of which now hung the tag of murderer and a sentence to a high-walled penitentiary for the remainder of his life.

No matter that the judge had been biased and self-serving, that the jury had been stacked against him, that a witness who could have helped his cause had mysteriously disappeared. All that had been ignored by those whom he'd expected to stand by him; instead, they simply forgot or disregarded all of the years he had served them as an honest, reliable town marshal. It was only too evident that the toes he was treading upon were those of men far too powerful to permit a small town lawman to upset their schemes. It was far better that one nonentity be put away where he could do no harm than have their existence disturbed.

But Matt guessed he'd had the last laugh. Knowing the ropes — having made the journey to the pen himself many times when conducting a prisoner to that institution — he had managed his escape without injuring the young deputy in whose charge he had been placed, and had headed north on a trail calculated to fool the posse that was certain to be organized and sent in pursuit. He had followed that course for a time and then doubled back, heading due south for Mexico.

Now the border was only a day or less away. Once across it, he'd be safe from

Deputy U.S. Marshal Fred Larkin or any other lawman who might be looking for him. That realization narrowed Kollister's eyes and drew his thick, overhanging brows together as he considered the town coldly.

He could see no telegraph wires entering the settlement, so it appeared that Larkin could not have dispatched a wire to the local lawman advising him to be on the lookout. And it was doubtful that, in the time elapsed since he had broken free of the deputy, a letter or a wanted circular detailing his crime and bearing his likeness could have reached the place.

But, Matt thought wryly, anything was possible. A month ago who would have believed that he would have found himself hurrying to lose his identity on the yonder side of the Mexican border?

One thing *was* certain — the growing crowd in the street, now looking expectantly in his direction, was waiting for someone. Like as not they figured him for someone else, but Matt wasn't sure that he wanted to risk it being a coincidence. He was too close now to his goal. It might be smarter to wheel the bay about on the bridge, swing wide of the town and continue on his way.

Kollister shrugged off the impulse. If the town lawman was waiting for him, there'd

11

be no crowd standing in the street. Also, if he made a run for it now, it would be a dead giveaway to Shoham's marshal that he was a wanted man, and a chase would certainly follow. Matt didn't want that — he had already made up his mind that he was not going to be caught and taken back to serve his years behind the grim, rock walls of a penitentiary for a crime he had not committed. So far he had encountered no opposition or problems on his flight to Mexico, and that was the way he wanted it to stay. In his mind he was finished with ever again being a lawman, and his estimation of law and order in general had fallen to a low level. But he also wanted no part of shooting it out with any man wearing a star, who would, after all, only be doing his sworn duty.

Such applied doubly to Fred Larkin, but Kollister was determined to let no one stand between him and his crossing the line into Mexico, even if it was his old friend who overtook and confronted him. He didn't know just what he'd do if he didn't use his gun, but he'd manage somehow.

Drawing himself up, dropping a hand on the butt of the pistol riding high on his hip, Matt Kollister raked the bay lightly with his spurs and put the big gelding into motion.

Whatever it was all about he'd soon know, he thought as he brushed his hat forward to better shield his eyes from the noon sun and continued on across the bridge.

## 2

He was crossing the west branch of the stream, Matt realized, noting the sparkle of water of the adjoining branch veering off through the brush and trees to his left. Shoham lay in the hollow formed by the division, and his initial impression of the town had been fairly accurate. It was of fair size, with a single wide street, and it was evident that it offered most everything those persons living there or passing through might need.

A barbershop with an adjoining doctor's office stood first to his right at the beginning of the line of buildings. Next came a small, somewhat run-down hostelry bearing the name Palace Hotel. Beside it was the Trail's End Saloon, after which, in a succession of irregular sizes, followed Ferlin's Gun & Saddle Shop, the Alamo Hotel and Restaurant, Wheeler's Meat Market, and another saloon designated as the Bonanza. Beyond and back a short distance from the road which continued on to the south was an ornate, two-storied structure that could only be a bawdy house.

First on the opposite side of the dusty lane, which was shaded here and there by large cottonwood trees, was a clothing store. The sign extending across the front of the building at roof level declared it to be The Emporium, Levi Marcus, Prop. Craig's General Store adjoined, after which came Yates's Feed & Seed Store, the Bullhead Saloon, a small, narrow structure that appeared to be the jail and the local lawman's quarters and lastly Salem's Livery Barn, a broad, sprawling building with a corrugated tin roof that shone like new silver in the driving summer sun. Scattered among these principal establishments were various small firms.

The residential area appeared to lie to the west of the business district. Kollister could see two dozen or more houses sprinkled capriciously about on a grassy flat. Near the center, a squat white church with its cross silhouetted against the steel blue of the sky overlooked all.

Buggies and saddle horses were drawn up to the hitchracks along the street, or were halted in the wagon yards of the various establishments. In addition to the crowd facing him expectantly, other persons had now appeared in the doorways and at the windows of the buildings, and were looking on.

"Sure am glad to see you!" a man in the forefront of the gathering called out as Kollister drew the bay to a stop. "Been waiting most of the morning."

Matt studied the speaker expressionlessly. Somewhere in the crowd a cautious voice seemed to say, *You reckon this is him? Looks more like a gun-shark to me.*

"We got the word you was headed this way," the man who had greeted him continued. "I'm John Craig. Can say we're all mighty relieved you're finally here." Evidently the owner of the town's general store, Craig took a step forward and extended his arm.

Kollister accepted the merchant's welcome with a brief handshake and a nod, feeling it best to play it cool until he knew exactly what it was all about. Raising his head, he let his eyes run the crowd. It was obviously a committee of some kind, organized to meet a man they were expecting — and were pleased to see. They appeared to be merchants, judging from their attire, and there was one woman among them — tall, dark-haired, with light eyes and calm, even features, and a figure that the straight-lined calico dress she was wearing could not conceal.

The careful voice in the crowd spoke again: *He's got the look for damn sure! I'm betting nobody ever pushed him around.*

"I'd like to introduce the rest of the folks who sent for you," Craig said, half turning. "Lady there is Seera Ford. Runs the Alamo Hotel and Restaurant, where you'll be staying and boarding if it's jake with you."

The woman smiled a cool, reserved welcome. Matt responded, wondering if Seera Ford had a husband. Craig had said she operated the hotel and restaurant, which led him to think she could be a widow; no woman with her looks and bearing could ever escape marriage, he was certain.

"Man next to her is Ferlin Webb. Then there's Simon Deal — owns the Trail's End Saloon, Oren Yates of the feedstore, Hank Beatty who owns the Bullhead Saloon, Tom Salem, Seth Wheeler, and Bert McAdams. His place is the Bonanza." Craig paused and gestured toward a slightly-built man hurriedly approaching. "Fellow just coming up is Levi Marcus. He's got the clothing store . . . You're a mite late, Levi."

"Had a customer," Marcus replied and bobbed to Kollister.

"Now, we ain't everybody that's been waiting and hoping you'd get here," Craig continued, "but we're the ones that've done the hollering."

"And you sure couldn't've got here at a better time," said Salem, a lean, cadaverous oldster with a hawk-like face. He glanced about the street as if wanting to be sure his words were not heard beyond the immediate gathering. "No, sir, you sure couldn't."

"Fact is," the man called Beatty — dark, somewhere in his mid-twenties and with a worried look on his face — added, "I'd say you got here right in the nick of time."

Matt decided he had let things ride far enough. These men, apparently the town's council, were expecting someone else, certainly not him, as there was no lawman in the party. Pushing his hat to the back of his head, he wiped the sweat from his face with a forearm, and shook his head.

"Don't know what this is all about, but I'm afraid that you —"

"Hell, I reckon we've all gone and forgot our manners," Craig broke in apologetically. He was dressed neatly in a gray business suit, and despite the heat was wearing a stiff collar and a necktie. "Let's get in out of the sun and do our talking."

Kollister remained motionless in the

saddle. "I think you best hear me out first
—"

"Nope, that can wait till we get where it's
a mite cooler," Craig said flatly.

A murmur of agreement seconded his
statement. Craig smiled up at Matt. "Just
climb down off your saddle and we'll ad-
journ to Seera's restaurant. Tom, you mind
seeing to the marshal's horse?"

Kollister frowned as he came off the bay.
They thought he was a marshal! He paused
as the members of the committee moved
slowly toward the Alamo Hotel, all taking
their time so as not to outdistance him. A
man who had been summoned by Tom
Salem, the stable owner, was reaching for
the headstall of the bay and was preparing
to lead the horse away. Matt started to halt
him, to again point out that an error was
being made, but Craig and the others were
almost to the hotel. Shrugging, Kollister let
it ride. He'd clear it all up after they were
inside Seera Ford's restaurant.

Moving on, Matt caught up with the party
as they reached the front of the Alamo. All
paused briefly; then, led by the woman, they
entered the lobby of the hostelry and followed her through a portiered doorway into
the restaurant, which occupied a large
adjoining room. Two tables had been placed

together near an open window in the back. Halting beside them, Seera beckoned to the men.

"We can sit here. It will be cooler."

There was a nodding of assents as the party filed past her. Kollister hesitated when he drew abreast of the woman and gave her a close, direct look, struck more so than before by her quiet beauty. She returned his attention with her restrained smile, and he continued on to the chair being reserved for him by John Craig, where he again paused until Seera had sat down.

"First off," he said, at once taking the lead, "you folks have made a mistake. Tried to tell you —"

"How so?" Oren Yates demanded almost angrily as Kollister settled onto his chair. Yates looked more to be a farmer, scrubbed and clean after a day in the fields, than a merchant. "One of my boys spotted you up the way late yesterday. Seen you making camp. Figured you was the fellow we been waiting for and rode on ahead to let us know."

Matt gave that thought. It explained the welcoming committee in the street and verified what he'd concluded earlier — they assumed he was someone else.

"Coffee'll be here in a minute," Seera announced, motioning to an elderly woman in a white Mother Hubbard dress who apparently served as a waitress.

"Cold beer'd be more fitting," said McAdams, a squat, tough-visaged individual, mopping at his face and neck with a handkerchief.

Seera's lips parted again into a soft smile. "Now, Bert, I don't serve liquor and you don't serve meals — that's our agreement."

McAdams grinned. "I reckon it is. Was only doing a bit of wishing."

Craig had rocked back and was studying Kollister. "A man looking at you can see you're who and what we figure you are —"

"Ain't only that," Yates added. "You can see the holes on the pocket of your shirt where you been wearing a star. Cloth ain't faded none there, either. That's plenty good proof you're a lawman, unless you're wearing somebody else's shirt."

Matt smiled. "Nope, it's my shirt for sure. But I'm not the man you think I am."

Kollister saw disappointment spread across Seera Ford's face. Her eyes closed tight as if she were in pain. Craig, frowning darkly, glanced around the table at the other merchants.

"You ain't a lawman — the one we've been asking for?"

21

Matt shook his head. "No —"

"But showing up here, and them holes in your shirt where you been wearing a badge — like Yates said, you've got to be a lawman!"

"I'm a lawman all right," Kollister said, but quickly caught himself. "Or was — once."

"Knew it!" Simon Deal, owner of the Trail's End, said, slapping his hands together. "You got the look."

"Maybe, but I'm not one now, and I don't aim to be one ever again," Kollister said, his hooded gaze on Seera Ford. "I'm mighty sorry to disappoint you, but I'm headed for Mexico and I don't figure to waste much time getting there."

The men exchanged glances. Craig sighed heavily and Seera Ford, shoulders going down, turned to Matt.

"We — we're sorry to hear that, Mr. —"

"Kollister — Matt Kollister."

"— Mr. Kollister," she finished. "We've been waiting and hoping for someone like you to come. We need help, bad."

Seera paused as the elderly waitress appeared bringing a tray of mugs filled with steaming liquid.

"Here's our coffee. Won't you be our guest long enough to hear what we have to say?"

Kollister considered the woman quietly: She had a small, pert nose and her mouth was firm but perfectly shaped, but it was her smile that caught and held his attention. There was a tinge of sadness to it, as if life had dealt her far more than her share of trouble.

"Sure," he said, relaxing in his chair.

Everyone was silent while the waitress placed the mugs of coffee on the table and centered a pitcher of cream and a bowl of sugar. When she had finished and was moving away, John Craig took up his cup and had a swallow. Then, with the container poised in his hand, he laid his gaze on Matt.

"I reckon you're wondering why we're trying so hard to get a lawman."

"Trying?" Kollister questioned. "Shouldn't be too hard to do."

"Has been for us. We've been looking for a long time. Fact is, we started writing the U.S. Marshal in Washington months ago asking for a deputy. All we ever got was promises."

"We had you figured for that deputy," Simon Deal explained. "That's how come all the foofaraw. We all had it in mind that Washington had finally got around to listening to us."

Matt glanced through the restaurant

window to the jail on the opposite side of the street. "You saying you don't have a lawman? No town marshal or constable? A place this size — I can see the jail — seems you ought —"

"Guess you can say that's what's at the bottom of our problem," Craig cut in.

"For certain," Seth Wheeler declared, tossing off the last of his coffee. "Expect we'd have a lawman here right now if it wasn't for Huckaby and his bunch."

"Huckaby?" Matt echoed.

"Hiram Huckaby — rancher east of here. Big man in these parts. Heads up the Cattleman's Association along with a half dozen homesteaders who've lined up with him because they're scared not to.

"He's always had a hankering to run the town and because we've fought it, he lets his crowd run wild around here. They ride in high-handed as you please, acting like they own everything, tearing up the place and slapping folks around and —"

"Best thing you can do is forget the U.S. Marshal and call in the sheriff of whatever county this is —"

"Can't," MacAdams said bluntly. "I mean, we ain't in no county. We're setting a-straddle the line — half in New Mexico Territory, half in the State of Texas, and

24

neither one of them'll take the responsibility of looking after us until they get the boundary dispute worked out."

"We're what they call unorganized territory, and it's been that way for near six years now," Tom Salem said. "I mean, they've been trying to straighten it out for us that long."

"And it'll probably be another six before they get done wrassling over it," Craig said. "Meantime we're having to set here trying to make a living, sweating out every day, caught between a rock and a hard place."

Kollister frowned, not certain if the remark had deeper meaning.

"He's threatened to burn down the town," Wheeler said, "and we're about halfway expecting it."

"Was that cowboy bunch that killed Seera's husband," McAdams offered. "We ain't never found out which one of them it was that put the bullet in Dan, but we know one of them did."

Matt turned his attention to the woman. "Mighty sorry to hear about that."

Seera Ford's shoulders stirred. "It was a time ago. Doesn't hurt much now."

There were a few moments of silence, and then Matt asked, "Have you tried hiring a lawman?"

"Sure have," Craig replied promptly. "Not once, but several times over the last couple of years. Trouble is, Huckaby's crowd runs them off — almost before they get their star pinned on.

"We done the same thing once when Huckaby sent a fellow in here to take the job. We found out he was one of Huckaby's bunch, worked for one of the ranchers. We managed to get rid of him — with a little help."

Kollister studied his empty cup. "This Huckaby, has he got some hired guns working for him or is it just his regular crew that's giving you trouble?"

Craig shifted his glance to Salem. "Tom says that a couple of them are shooters."

Salem nodded. "One's called Charlie Marshall. I seen him over in Fort Worth a couple of years back. Had a reputation then as a fast gun and could be hired out. Then there's a couple others, Ed Waggoner and George Schultz. Both plenty bad, not that the rest of the crowd — Huckaby likes to call them his Enforcers — ain't meaner'n hell. Sorry about that, Seera."

The woman smiled. Ferlin Webb said, "For my money, the worst of the bunch, when it comes down to pure, mean cussedness, is Travis Huckaby — old Hiram's son.

Ain't any of that bunch worse'n him. Why, he come into my store a couple of weeks ago and just plain tore up the place. Just looking around, he claimed."

The elderly waitress appeared, this time bringing an enamel pot of fresh coffee. She made the rounds of the table, silently refilling the empty cups. Outside in the street there was the sudden pound of hoofs as a rider in a great hurry rushed by.

"Expect that gives you a fair idea of the fix we're in," Craig said, then added, "Guess it explains, too, why we're mighty anxious to hire you on."

"And if you're interested," Oren Yates said, "we'd be willing to pay you whatever wages you wanted — within reason, of course."

"We ain't got a lot of money but I reckon we can meet your price," Salem assured Matt.

Seera Ford pushed forward on her chair. Her mouth was tightly set as she shook her head. "I don't think we're being fair to Mr. Kollister by not telling him everything." She paused, transferred her attention to Matt. "Our trouble with Hiram Huckaby and the ranchers is only half of what we're up against. The truth is —"

"Truth is we've got outlaw trouble, too,"

John Craig cut in. "It's mainly my fault because it was me that talked folks around here into letting them hang around. I figured they'd mean a lot of extra cash business, which was something we could all use."

The store owner hesitated, began to toy with his cup of coffee. Kollister considered him briefly; he'd been right about the remark Craig made earlier: it had had deeper meaning.

"They were all right at first," Yates admitted, "behaved themselves and done plenty of spending. But that's all changed. Hardly a week goes by that there ain't been a couple of break-ins and robberies. They been sort of like cats — we let them stick their noses inside the door, and next thing we knew they'd moved in all the way."

"And they ain't moved on like they was supposed to," Levi Marcus said. "They just keep hanging around. Only now they're costing us business instead of helping it."

"So what we're wanting from a lawman is for him to get Huckaby off our backs and the outlaw bunch out of our town," Craig said. "Now, I wasn't intending to hide the pea from you by not mentioning the outlaws. You being a lawman, I figured they'd be no big problem to you. And, I'm plenty

28

sure they wouldn't because you're just the man we're looking for."

Kollister stared off into the street. "Can't figure how you can say that. You don't know me — never even heard of me before. What makes you think I won't cut and run when Huckaby and his crew come down on me — or that I won't back off from those outlaws?"

"Well, I'd bet my bottom dollar that you wouldn't," Yates drawled. "Sure I don't know you, but I'm a pretty fair judge of men and you ain't the knuckling down kind. I reckon you never was and you never will be."

"And if you'll take the job, it'll be you with the say-so all the way," Craig added. "There'd be none of us butting in telling you how to run the show. You'd be the town marshal, the law, and we'd back you all the way."

"And you won't have no trouble putting on a deputy if you're of a mind," Yates said. "Once word gets around that we've hired on a marshal that ain't scared to stand up to anybody, no matter who, there'll be plenty of men willing to go to work for you."

Matt listened idly, his attention on Seera Ford. He'd been right about her, too; she was a widow. The woman glanced up at that moment, caught his eyes upon her. She smiled and looked away.

"Is there anything at all we can say or offer to get you to take the job?" Bert McAdams asked. "Like you've already been told, the money ain't no special problem."

Kollister shook his head. "Seems to me your giving me the job is sort of like a man buying a horse blind-folded."

"Maybe looks that way to you, but that ain't the way we see it," said Levi Marcus, speaking for only the second time since the meeting began. "It ain't hard to tell good merchandise from the poor quality stuff. Same goes for a man."

"Levi's right," Craig said, dabbing at the sweat on his forehead with a handkerchief. "We're so sold on you being our man that we ain't even interested in asking you why you took off your badge and are heading for Mexico. Appears to me that ought to prove what we think of you."

Matt swung his eyes to Seera Ford. She was studying him hopefully, anxiously.

"Please," she said, before he could speak, "please consider helping us before you say no."

# 3

Seera looked away and Matt again swung his attention to the street. The townspeople of Shoham were in desperate need, there was no doubt of that. And he could help — but did he want the job as the town's savior? He'd vowed never to pin on another star and accept the responsibilities of a lawman; the rewards were too small, and he was not about to once more lay himself open for the hurt and disillusionment he'd experienced at Tiuga.

But maybe this was different. He'd be a lawman for only a short while, just long enough to clear up the problems between the people of Shoham, the outlaws, and the Huckaby cattleman faction. Such a job would require a firm stand on the part of the man wearing the star, and a proclamation that he'd stand for no foolishness and was to be obeyed to the last letter. In this case it would mean ordering the outlaws to move on and seeing that they did, as well as bringing the cattlemen and the people of the town together for an understanding. Once that was accomplished, he could ride on. He was but a short day from the Mexican border, and if Fred Larkin picked up his trail and put in an appearance, there would likely be time to mount up and make it to the border before the marshal learned for certain that he was in Shoham.

But coming down to the root of it, why should he concern himself with the town's needs? They had been looking for a lawman for a long time; it wouldn't hurt to let them search a bit further. Matt gave that thought. So far, they had failed; no man wanted the job and those who had accepted had been driven off by the cattlemen's Enforcers.

Since the U.S. Marshal's office in far-off Washington had turned a deaf ear to their pleas, and they could get no help from the capitals of New Mexico or Texas, Shoham could very well stay a no-man's-land, compelled to stand or fall on its own.

Could he, in all conscience, turn his back on these people? Could *any* man with an inherent feeling for law and order coursing through his veins do so? Responsibility was a deep-seated thing, especially for a man who had worn a star with pride all of his working life!

"There's a few things you'd best know first," Matt said, turning back to Craig and the others gathered around the tables. "I —"

"We don't have to know nothing!" Salem cut in, all but shouting the words as he realized the import of Kollister's statement. "We're wanting you to hire on no matter what."

"Hear me out," Matt insisted quietly. "I want you to know what I might have to do, and understand the reason."

Kollister's gaze shifted to Seera Ford. She was regarding him intently, a smile on her lips. Her eyes had become a clean, clear blue beyond reach of the harsh sunlight, and her hair was even darker than it had looked in the street.

"I come from a town up Colorado way — Tiuga, it's called. Was the town marshal there for quite a few years. It's a fine place, and I thought folks there were my friends. Found out different when it came down to their taking a stand."

"Like Tom said, there still ain't no need," Craig commented, shaking his head.

Kollister raised his cup, had a swallow of coffee. Back in the kitchen area of the restaurant there was a loud clatter as something was dropped. No one seemed to notice.

"I want this out in the open," Matt continued, setting his cup down. "I want you to be sure of who you're hiring — a man who escaped with a murder charge and conviction hanging over him and who has a Deputy U.S. Marshal on his trail."

Craig frowned. Oren Yates brushed nervously at his mustache and said, "Except there was a good reason for whatever you done."

"This U.S. Marshal, where is he now?" Seth Wheeler wanted to know.

"Shook him yesterday. Was in rough country east of here, so it'll take him a while to pick up my tracks, but he will. Name's Fred Larkin, and he's an old friend of mine. He was the man who got me started as a lawman."

Kollister glanced about the circle, touched each member of the committee with his eyes. "Want this made clear: if Larkin shows up — and he will, sooner or later — I'll have to pull out, make a run for the border. I won't let him take me back, and I won't shoot it out with him."

"We understand," Craig said, nodding to the others who signified their agreement in a like manner.

"This trouble, the murder charge — you care to tell us about it?" Beatty said hesitantly. "Not necessary if you'd rather not."

"No reason to keep it quiet," Kollister replied indifferently. "It was over a shipment of gold from a mine, about forty thousand dollars' worth. The stagecoach carrying it was held up. Both the driver and the shotgun messenger were killed. No passengers aboard, so there were no witnesses to who did it.

"Happened right close to my town so I naturally got mixed up in trying to run down the killer — or killers — who took the gold. A couple of days after I started prying around, I got word from the higher-ups to back off, leave it alone. They said they were doing their own investigating.

"That was jake with me, and I did just what they said — backed off. But both the stagecoach driver and the guard were friends of mine, and when I saw that there wasn't any investigating being done at all, I started out on my own again. Turned up some surprises right quick."

"Surprises? Meaning what?" Wheeler wanted to know.

"Things that made it plenty clear the robbery was all cut and dried and that a couple of the big muckety-mucks — the same men who'd ordered me to keep hands off — were in it clear up to their hatbands."

"You saying the men who held up the coach and killed the driver and guard were the same ones who told you to back off?"

"Not exactly, but they had it done. Had a man or men waiting in a narrow pass folks call Deadwood Canyon. It's not far out of Tiuga. After I'd dug around a bit I got to figuring that a fellow right there in town — a cardsharp named Stryker — had a hand in it. All of a sudden he had too much money, and it was known that he had friends high up.

"I didn't have any idea who the man was that sided him — or even for sure that there was somebody else — but I figured I could get that out of Stryker once I had him nailed down, which I was able to do after talking to a few people and finding out some things that backed up my suspicions.

"Anyway, I went to arrest him and found him in the lobby of the hotel talking to a fellow I'd never seen before. When I told Stryker what I knew, and that I was taking him in for murder and robbery, he went for his belly-gun and I had to shoot."

"Kill him?" Craig asked.

Kollister brushed at the sweat on his face,

glanced at Seera Ford, and nodded. "No choice."

"Was your right," Tom Salem declared. "Was him or you."

There was a mutter of agreement from the others. Matt nodded again and continued. "Right then the high-ups began cracking down on me. They were scared I was getting too close and knew too much. They had me arrested for murder. The gun Stryker pulled mysteriously disappeared along with the jasper he had been talking to — my only witness.

"I got hauled up before a judge who was either in on the gold robbery or was protecting somebody, and a jury that was made up of men who had been paid off or were afraid to buck the big politicians. They listened to what I had to say, but I had nobody to back up my story and nobody in the town stepped forward to testify on my behalf — despite my record as a good lawman. They just believed I was lying about Stryker drawing a pistol. Then, when the court brought in a stranger who swore he'd been with Stryker the day of the robbery — in a town a hundred miles away — I figured I was up against it.

"The judge sentenced me to the pen for the rest of my life after the jury found me guilty. I looked for the town to step in then for sure and back me, but it didn't. I'm pretty sure they believed what I had said, that Stryker drew a gun and that there was a witness — and that I was being framed by some powerful men who couldn't afford to let me dig any deeper into the gold robbery — but at a time like that folks just sort of feel they have to look out for themselves and not take any chances on getting in trouble."

"You go to the pen and then escape?" Simon Deal wanted to know.

Matt shook his head. "Was on the way there. I tricked the deputy and escaped. Did a bit of riding about to throw them off my trail, then headed for Mexico — which brought me here."

"Your friend, that U.S. Marshal, Larkin," Hank Beatty said, "didn't he stand by you?"

"Wasn't around. Was off somewhere in Montana, tracking down a killer. He didn't come in on it until I'd been sentenced and was on my way to the pen."

"Well, the way I see it," Tom Salem declared, "you got a mighty raw deal. I sure can't fault you none for busting loose and heading for Mexico."

Kollister stirred. "Don't like being against the law. Always respected it and did my best to uphold it, but I couldn't swallow what was being jammed down my throat. Thought I'd hole up in Mexico till things had blown over — a couple of years, maybe. Then I'd go back and try to track down that witness and clear myself."

"The thing to do, all right," Craig said, "but we'd sure like for you to take over the job here as town marshal. What you've told us don't change our minds one whit."

"For a fact," Yates said, looking around the tables at the others for confirmation.

After a moment Seera Ford said, "How long will you stay?"

Kollister shrugged. "Till I can get things straightened out for you here, or till Fred Larkin shows up — whichever happens first."

"Let's hope he never comes!" Oren Yates said fervently. "But just a few days'll be a big help. Way I figure it, it won't take you long to set things straight for us."

"Aim to try," Matt replied.

"Then I guess we got ourselves a marshal," John Craig said, smiling.

"Reckon you have," Kollister agreed, pushing back his chair and getting to his feet. "Just give me the keys to my office and the jail and I'll go to work."

# 4

Matt turned to Seera Ford as the others noisily shoved back their chairs and rose. "Seems I remember Craig saying I'd be boarding here in your hotel."

The woman nodded, smiled as she drew herself erect. "I'll arrange everything," she said, and shifted her attention to Salem. "Tom, I expect you'll be looking after Mr. Kollister's —"

"Matt." Kollister interrupted.

Seera smiled again. "— after Matt's horse. I'll be obliged if you'll bring in his saddlebags and the like."

The livery stable man bobbed. "I'll do just that," he said, and added to Kollister, "Don't worry none about the bay, Marshal, I'll see he gets good care."

*Marshal.* To be addressed as such sounded good again to Matt. "I'll appreciate it," he said and turned for the doorway leading into the restaurant from the hotel's lobby as the party began to break up.

"Jail's right across the street," Craig said, stepping in beside him. "Office is in the front; cells are in the back — only got two."

Matt made his way through the lobby out onto the hotel's porch and crossing to its edge, halted. Craig and Beatty paused beside him.

"Place's been locked up for a few months," Craig said, digging into the pocket of his coat apparently in search of a key. "Going to take a mite of cleaning and dusting."

Kollister was only half listening, more aware of the others who had attended the meeting moving by him with their murmurs of encouragement and good wishes. They headed back to their respective establishments, and he nodded briefly to each.

"I'll open up for you," Craig said. He came down off the Alamo's porch and started across the street.

Kollister, following a step behind with Beatty at his shoulder, slowed as two men emerged from the Trail's End, by far the largest and most pretentious of the town's saloons. Matt's jaw hardened as he considered them.

"Sam Vickers," he murmured, fixing his eyes on the taller of the two, a lanky redhead

41

who was now watching him with amused eyes. "Wondered what'd happened to him."

"How's that?" Beatty said, not hearing the lawman's low words.

"Vickers, the hardcase with red hair that just came out of that saloon. He's wanted in a dozen or more places, near as I recall. Same goes for the man with him — Calico Hays — and the one coming through the door now, Pete Irby. These the outlaws that're giving you trouble?"

Beatty nodded. "Some of them. Vickers there is the ramrod. Would seem you already know them."

"From way back," Matt said, moving on.

"They was all right when they first rode into here," Beatty said. "Behaved themselves and spent a lot of money with us — ain't that right, John?"

They reached the front of the jail and halted. Craig, standing in the doorway of the small structure, frowned. "Ain't what right?"

"Was saying Vickers and his bunch were all right when they first come here."

"They were," Craig agreed in a positive way. "Paid cash money for everything they bought, never caused us no trouble except maybe a fracas now and then down at the Palace Hotel — they got a little bar there in a back room. And when they did bust up something in one of the places, Sam Vickers seen to it that the damage was taken care of. Way they was then's the reason I recommended to everybody that we let them hang around."

Matt's gaze had shifted to the saloon at the opposite end of the street from the Trail's End — the Bonanza. Four men were now in evidence there, having come from the saloon's interior and taken up indolent positions along its front wall.

Matt swore softly. "You folks've got them all roosting down here for sure," he said in a marveling tone, and ticked off those names of the quartet that he knew: "Billy Blue and the Mex, Copio Benavidez — and that fast-gun killer, Cherokee Smith, who claims nobody can stand up to him. Fourth one's a stranger but I'll bet he's wanted in a lot of places, too. One thing certain, there's more owlhoots collected in this one place than anywhere else I've been — except for the pen."

"Good reason for it," Beatty said. "We're close to Mexico. Men like Vickers and Blue and such can hang around here and still have time to duck across the border if a U.S. Marshal shows up looking for them."

"You figure you'll have much trouble driving them out?" Craig wondered, and added morosely, "We — I made a mistake letting them hole up here."

Beatty shrugged. "Ain't sure we could've made them move on if we'd wanted. Had Old Man Finney wearing the marshal's badge then, and all he was good for was jailing drunks."

"Going to take some shooting now, I expect," Matt agreed.

Matt had turned fully about. Sam Vickers with Hays and Pete Irby had left their places in front of the Trail's End and were sauntering across the street. They reached the small landing in front of the jail and halted. Vickers, folding his arms across his chest, rocked back on his heels.

"Howdy," he said with a broad grin.

Kollister nodded coldly. The outlaw shrugged, spat into the dust.

"Ain't sure where I recollect you from," Vickers said, "but it was some place up the way, and you was the marshal."

"Colorado, town called Tiuga. I ran you out."

The redhead nodded. "Sure, I'm remembering now. You was lucky because I was feeling poorly. Mind speaking your name?"

"Kollister."

"Yeh, that's it. Kollister. And you had

44

yourself a friend helping — a sheriff I think he was. Skinny little jasper, little but hell for stout, as the saying goes. Expect he's a bit long in the tooth by now; and he was graying out plenty then."

"He gets around," Kollister said in the same cold voice.

"Yep, I'll bet he does. He's that kind," Vickers said and glanced at Craig. "He going to be your marshal?" he asked, jerking a thumb at Matt.

The merchant nodded. "Taking over soon as I can swear him in."

"Do tell," the outlaw said, and grinned at his two friends. "Well, I hope you know what you're doing, Mister Mayor. Things've been running pretty smooth without no badge-toter. Sure don't see no reason for bringing one in now."

When both Beatty and Craig pointedly made no reply, Matt said, "Expect they've got plenty of reasons."

"We ain't done nothing," Calico Hays declared defensively. "We're just living here, taking it easy."

"Knowing you and your kind, I find that plenty hard to believe."

"Just like a damn lawman!" Vickers cut in. "You got your mind all made up about fellows like me and my boys. You don't think we can go straight when we want to."

Matt shook his head slowly. "Nope, I sure don't."

The easy, bantering manner Sam Vickers had assumed at the start had now vanished, and a sort of tension had settled over him and the men with him.

"Well, you're barking up the wrong tree, mister! And I'm telling you something right here and now: Don't you go trumping up anything bad on us or —"

"Or what?" Kollister pressed gently when the outlaw broke off.

Vickers was a rigid shape in the streaming sunlight for a long breath, and then looked off down the street with a shrug. Several persons, sensing trouble of some kind, had come out into the open and were watching intently.

"Just you don't try nothing," the outlaw finished.

"I figure to do whatever's needful," Matt said with a promising sort of smile. "Best thing I can say to you right now is make yourself scarce while you've got time. There's going to be some changes."

"You ordering us out of town?" Irby demanded.

"Good way to figure it. If you —"

"What the hell you doing way down here,

46

anyway?" Vickers interrupted. "Seems to me you come a mighty long way just to take on a two-bit job like being marshal in this dump."

"Maybe he got hisself fired," Calico Hays suggested. "Maybe he got so high and mighty that them folks up there in that town where he was the law took his star and sent him packing."

"Whatever," Kollister replied evenly, "I don't put it down as any of your business. Point is, I'm here now, and I'll be running this town. You best take my advice and move on."

Vickers hawked and spat into the dust again. He glanced at Hays and Irby, then let his eyes travel on to the men standing in front of the Bonanza.

"This ain't Colorado, mister," he drawled, and pivoting, struck off down the street with Hays and Irby at his shoulders.

Motionless, silent, Matt watched them depart, heading apparently for the Palace Hotel and its bar. He was in for trouble, that was certain. Vickers and his bunch, total number still unknown, would be hard to root out — but it could be done, and he would do it. A sort of wry satisfaction stirred through Matt Kollister as he faced up to the problem. If —

"Expect you'd like to go inside and look over your office."

At John Craig's somewhat tentative words, Matt wheeled and stepped up into the small room, which was laden with trapped heat.

"Yeh," he answered. "Sooner we get things underway, the better I'll like it."

# 5

"Hotter'n hell in here," Hank Beatty muttered.

Hurrying on past Kollister, the saloon man opened a door in the rear wall that led into the adjoining room where the cells — a large iron cage partitioned in the center — had been constructed. Raising the solitary window in the narrow hallway fronting the cells, he heaved a sigh as a rush of fresh air greeted him.

"Reckon that'll help a little," he said.

Back in the office, Matt was glancing about. There was a desk with its customary swivel chair, and a gun rack on the wall behind them that was empty. Benches that lined two sides of the office were piled with yellowing newspapers, magazines, old clothing and empty liquor bottles — all apparently collected by someone intending to clean the place but who for some reason was interrupted before the removal of the trash could be effected.

Kollister's eyes paused on a large calendar supplied by a St. Louis feed company. It pictured a man clad in overalls, heavy shoes and a straw hat shaking hands with another who wore the distinct garb of a cattleman. The message being conveyed was apparently that both men were in accord as to the value of the company's product. The month on the calendar was long past.

"Been some time since this office was used," Matt said, crossing to the desk.

"Quite a spell, all right," Craig agreed. Stepping up to the calendar, he ripped off the expired sheets and added them to the trash on the benches.

"Be glad to send over my swamper and have him do some cleaning," Beatty offered. He had removed his hat and was scrubbing fingers in his sweat-dampened hair as he sought to enjoy the slight breeze drifting through the building.

Kollister shrugged and, sweeping the dust off the chair with his hat, sat down. "Expect there's a broom around somewhere. Can take care of it myself later," he said, and pulled open the top drawer of the desk.

"Star in there somewhere," Craig said, looking over Matt's shoulder. "Recollect putting it —"

"Here," Kollister cut in. Picking up the five-pointed nickel badge, he pinned it onto his shirt pocket. "Guess you being the mayor, it'll be up to you to swear me in."

Craig smiled, rubbed at his jaw. "This mayor business — that's just some of Sam Vickers's talk. The town don't have one. It just happened that I sort of took charge of things a few years ago and've been running the town ever since. Is it necessary you be sworn in? I never done it to any of the others."

"Up to you — and the town," Kollister said. "All that's important is that I've got the authority to be your marshal."

"You've done got it!" Craig declared promptly. "We gave it to you back there in Seera Ford's restaurant, all of us."

"Makes it official then," Kollister said, continuing to browse through the drawer. He found nothing of interest and pushed the compartment shut.

Looking up at Craig, he continued, "I've met your outlaws, now what about the Huckaby crowd? When did they last come to town?"

Beatty nodded to Craig. "Can tell you that right quick — was a bit over a week ago. Three of them come into my place, started drinking and getting out of hand. Ended up with me and a fellow I hire to sort of keep order having to throw them out."

"They do much damage?"

"Some. Ain't worrying about that, though. It's that they said they'd be back and square up for what we done to them, that they wasn't letting nobody kick around anyone from the Diamond H — that's Huckaby's spread, by the way."

Kollister's attention had shifted to the window in the front wall of the office. Through its dust-flatted surface he could see the Palace Hotel on the opposite side of the street. Vickers, with half a dozen or more friends, was standing in the shade being thrown by the building.

"And you figure they will?"

"Hell, I'm dead sure of it!" Beatty said, putting on his hat. "Every time something like that's happened before, they've rode in and started trouble. I've been looking for them to show up every day and night since."

"How does it happen the outlaw bunch and Huckaby's cowhands — his Enforcers you called them — don't tangle? Looks to me like they'd meet up sooner or later."

"I reckon it's just one of them accident things," Beatty replied, "but some of it's probably because Vickers and them usually do their drinking at the Palace's bar while the cattleman crowd hangs out at the other saloons."

"Been some trouble down at Dolly's Place, that fancy house at the edge of town. They go at it nose to nose ever once in a while, but it don't get serious. Dolly knows how to handle them. Tells them if they don't straighten up they can't ever come back," Craig added.

"Usually works for a place like that," Matt said. "The ranchers still trade with you?"

"Some, but they're buying most of what they need over in Congerstown, east of here about thirty miles. Quite a drive, but I reckon Huckaby laid down the law about it and that's where they all go. Ain't but ten miles from his ranch to here, and the same, more or less, from the other spreads," Craig said, and paused to look out into the street.

"They come in here for what they have to have in a hurry, I guess, but things ain't comfortable when any of them are around. Sort of like we're all playing with matches around a keg of gunpowder," he continued after a few moments.

"And all I get's hard drinking and hell raising," Hank Beatty said.

A smile cracked Kollister's mouth. "That's the kind of business you're in, ain't it?" he commented dryly.

"Yeh, but I can do without the trouble that came along with them."

"Goes hand in hand with whiskey," Matt said. "Is Huckaby himself in on the hell raising, or is it only the hired help?"

"Usually the hired help with that no-account boy of his, Travis, leading the bunch," Beatty said. "I ain't seen old Hiram for weeks. Did see the daughter over at Levi Marcus's a few days back."

"Daughter?"

Beatty nodded. "Her name's Beth. Kind of a tomboy gal, a bit on the rough side. Guess you could say she's the son that Travis ain't. Nothing like him."

"That's for certain," Craig agreed. "She don't have any use for Travis at all, which ain't hard to understand. The fool stunts he's pulled not only around here but in a few other towns has damn nigh caused old Hiram to disown him. He's never been nothing but trouble."

"Figures," Beatty said. "Being the son of the biggest rancher in the country, he thinks he can get away with anything, and I reckon he usually does. Folks are just plain too scared to buck him — not only because he's a Huckaby, but on account of he goes kind of loco when he gets crossed, and there ain't no telling what he'll end up doing."

"Killed a man over in El Paso last year," Craig said. "Was over some woman. Hiram had quite a time getting him off. That El Paso marshal was all for stringing Travis up."

"And that ain't the first time Hiram's had to call in a favor from some of his big *politico amigos* to save Travis's neck —"

"And it ain't likely to be the last," Craig finished for the saloon man. "Boy's just naturally trouble no matter where he is. Expect Hiram's double sorry about his wife dying when she did. Could be the boy'd have turned out different if she'd been around to bring him up."

"I don't know about that," Hank Beatty said. "Some jaspers are just born bad, and they don't ever change, no matter what. Anyway, I'd like to ask you something, Marshal. What you said to Sam Vickers and the two with him about making themselves scarce while they still had time — you don't think that's all it'll take to make them move on, do you?"

Kollister shook his head. "Not Vickers for sure, but some of the others may take the hint and pull out. That'll trim the odds some."

"They're a mite long all right, about a dozen to your one and —" Craig said and broke off in mid-sentence, his gaze reaching through the streaky glass to the street. "Me and Hank was telling you about Travis Huckaby," he resumed after a moment. "Looks like you're going to get a chance to meet him first hand. Him and some of them gunmen Hiram hired on are coming this way."

# 6

Beatty pivoted, rushed to the doorway. "They're heading for my place!" he said in a taut voice. "That Diamond H bunch told me they'd come back and get even, and that's what Travis and them are aiming to do!"

Kollister rose and crossed quickly to the saloon man's side. "Stay in here," he said and stepped out into the open. "Both of you."

"But it's my place!" Beatty protested. "Seems I ought to —"

A shake of his head was the lawman's only reply. Halting on the landing fronting the jail, he threw his glance up the street, which was suddenly deserted. Five riders were approaching. They rode abreast, strung out arrogantly in a line that took up almost the entire width of the roadway. Matt swung his eyes to the front of the Palace Hotel where he'd last seen Vickers and several of his outlaw bunch. There was no sign of them; like the townspeople, they too had disappeared.

That reaction on the part of the outlaws puzzled Kollister and continued to strike him as strange. Why would hardcases like Vickers and those who ran with him take pains to avoid a confrontation with Huckaby's so-called Enforcers? Certainly Vickers and his crowd weren't the kind to turn tail and run without putting up a fight.

It could be explained, Matt reasoned after a moment, when you looked at it from the outlaws' point of view. They had a good thing going there in Shoham, or did at the start when the merchants agreed to let them hang around on promise of good behavior. But that had changed now, and there was no longer any reason for —

"One in the middle on the big chestnut with the fancy saddle — that's Travis," Craig's voice said from the doorway of the office.

Kollister brought his attention back to the oncoming riders. Travis Huckaby appeared to be in his mid-twenties. He had a dark, narrow face with small, quick eyes, and there was an air of hostility about him.

"Man to the left is Charlie Marshall — the gunfighter Salem told us about. That'n next to him is Ed Waggoner."

"I know him from up north," Matt said. "He's a cheap, two-bit back shooter. Who're the other two?"

"The one on the right wearing the old army hat, he's George Schultz — some folks call him Dutch. Buck Snapp's the last one."

"They the Enforcers?"

"Yeh, but there's a couple missing. McEvee and Chet Jones ain't along."

A silence followed the merchant's words, broken finally by Hank Beatty.

"What're you figuring to do?" he asked anxiously, leaning out of the doorway and craning his neck to see the front of his establishment next door.

"Depends on them," Kollister answered. Stepping down off the landing into the street, he placed himself in full view of Huckaby and the men with him.

The riders did not slow at his appearance but came steadily on, evidently secure in their belief that since no one had ever stood up to them before, there was no possibility of it now. Finally, they reached the Bullhead and swung up to the hitchrack fronting it. Immediately two men who were inside where they were apparently having themselves a drink exited hastily. Turning into the passageway that lay between the saloon and the adjacent building, Yates's Feed & Seed Store, they quickly vanished.

Travis Huckaby laughed and pointed at the hurrying figures. "Sure puts a man in mind of a couple of rats a-skedaddling out of a feed barn," he said as he drew to a halt; then, settling his attention on Kollister, he added, "Well, howdy do! What've we got here! A brand-new lawman!"

Charlie Marshall, a lean, slightly-built man wearing two guns in crossed belts, made no comment. Waggoner also remained silent, a frown puckering his browned features, but Schultz and Snapp both laughed.

"Sure enough," the latter man said. "What d'you reckon we ought to do with him, Travis?"

"Reckon we could tie him onto a horse and give him a ride out of town," Schultz suggested.

"Yep, expect we could," Huckaby agreed. "Seems we ought to give him a welcome party same as we done the others."

"Yeh — a welcome to get going," Dutch Schultz said, and broke into loud laughter.

Forearm on the horn of his silver-decorated saddle, Travis leaned forward. "Just what's your name, Sheriff?"

"Doubt if you ever heard it," Matt replied

60

coolly, "but it's Kollister. And I'm the town marshal, not the sheriff, or can't you read plain English? It's lettered out there on the star I'm wearing."

Travis drew up slowly, anger glittering in his dark eyes. "We got us a real smart-alecky one this time, boys. I reckon we ought to figure out something right special for him."

"Kollister," Ed Waggoner was repeating as he turned to Huckaby. A frown again pulled at his face, this time one of puzzlement. "I sure recollect that name from somewhere."

"Well, he can't be nothing much or I'd'a heard of him," Travis declared. "Now, let's get on with what we came here for, then we'll see to him. Dutch, you got them torches?"

"Sure have," Schultz answered. Half turning, he took from his saddlebags three short lengths of wood at the ends of which oil-soaked rags had been wrapped. Tossing one to Waggoner, he handed another to Snapp and retained the last for himself.

Huckaby nodded in satisfaction. Ignoring Matt, he leaned forward once more, but this time directed his voice to the dark interior of the Bullhead.

"Beatty!" he shouted. "You in there? Best you come out while you got a chance 'cause

61

I'm burning the place down. Warned you I
—"

"Beatty's not in there," Kollister cut in
quietly.

Huckaby's gaze shifted to the marshal.
"You doing his talking?"

"I am."

"Then you best roust him out and tell him
the reason I'm burning down his joint — in
case he don't recollect. He got real smart
with a couple of my friends, and I don't
stand for that from nobody. It's about time
him and the rest of the counter-jumpers in
this town learned that it don't pay to mess
with the Huckabys —"

"Happens it's the other way around, starting here and now," Kollister broke in, his
voice firm in the tense hush. "You and your
bunch are through hoorawing this town. I'm
giving you warning — I won't stand for any
more of your rough stuff."

"You won't stand for what?" Travis yelled,
his face growing darker as anger swept
through him. "You know who you're talking
to?"

Kollister nodded. "Makes no difference."

"Well, it sure will later! Go ahead, boys,
light them torches. Want a couple on the
roof, and one through the door. We'll sure'n
hell see who's running things around here."

Kollister's shoulders came forward slowly, and as Schultz and the other two men dug into their vest pockets for matches, he shook his head.

"Don't do it —"

Dutch Schultz hesitated, looked questioningly at Huckaby.

"Light it, damn you!" Travis shouted. "If this here tin-star tries to stop you, I'll take care of him!"

Schultz raked the match he held against the horn of his saddle and brought it to life. Snapp did the same, while at the opposite end of the party, Ed Waggoner already had his torch blazing.

"I'm telling you to forget it. Ride out of here before you're sorry." The lawman's voice was low, but carried distinctly along the empty street. The three men with their flaming torches again hesitated. Huckaby, his face livid, mouthed a curse at them and raised himself in the saddle, reaching for the pistol on his hip.

In that same moment, a gunshot echoed flatly along the street. Travis stiffened as blood blossomed on his chest. A strange, surprised look crossed his face. Twisting about, he fell heavily to the ground.

Frightened, the chestnut gelding Huckaby had been riding turned and trotted off as

Kollister took a step forward and flung a hurried, probing look along the street in hopes of locating the source of the shot. Buck Snapp's harsh voice brought him up short.

"You lousy, bushwhacking bastard! Had yourself a deputy holed up somewhere that was just waiting for the chance to potshot Travis!"

Kollister's jaw tightened. Settling back on his heels, he faced Snapp and the other Diamond H riders. Trouble with the ranch faction had come sooner than he'd expected, but he reckoned it didn't matter; trouble was trouble no matter when or where.

"I don't like your language," he said in a tight, suppressed tone. "And you're wrong — I don't have a deputy. And I don't know who did the shooting."

"You're a damn liar!" Snapp yelled shrilly, and made a stab for his gun.

Kollister rocked slightly to his right. His arm swept down and then up, all in little more than a blur. Metal glinted in his hand and the blast of the pistol he was suddenly holding sent a shock wave rolling along the silent street.

Buck Snapp jolted, buckled forward on his saddle, and began to fall. Kollister saw none of that; his narrowed eyes were on Charlie Marshall — reportedly the expert of the party, the premier shootist. Waggoner and Schultz were secondary. Both sat mouths agape, torches discarded and in the dust as they stared at the lawman.

"What's it to be?" Kollister pressed softly.

At that moment, Snapp struck the ground. His horse, taking a cue from Huckaby's, turned and fled a short distance up the street. Kollister's attention did not waver but remained riveted to the gunman.

Marshall, also motionless, had a palm resting on the butt of his left-hand pistol. Evidently the impulse to draw had deserted him when he saw how quickly Buck Snapp had gone down. Shrugging, he let his arm fall to his side.

"Not this time," he said in a low voice. "I do my shooting while I'm standing, not sitting." Cutting his horse about, he started back up the street. Schultz and Waggoner hesitated briefly and then turned to follow, trailed by Huckaby and Snapp's confused horses.

At once Hank Beatty hurried out into the open. "The bodies — yell at them, make them come back and take —"

"Never mind," Kollister said, studying the street now coming alive with excited townspeople for a possible clue to the hidden killer. "I'll see to them."

It was too late, of course, to do anything but ask questions and hope to find someone who had seen a puff of gunsmoke or heard the crack of the weapon used. The delay caused by the confrontation with Snapp and the other Huckaby riders had provided ample time for the bushwhacker to lose himself in the town.

"Was the damndest thing I ever seen, or didn't see!"

John Craig's voice broke into the lawman's thoughts. Coming about, Matt raised his pistol, punched out the spent cartridge and reloaded. A considerable crowd had now collected in front of the jail and more were hurrying along the street to join the gathering — some to stare at the bodies of Huckaby and Snapp, others to listen to Craig and Beatty.

"He had that gun out and shooting so fast a man couldn't see him doing it," Craig continued. "Sure did make that Charlie Marshall do some thinking."

"Next thing he was just standing there spraddle-legged, looking Travis and them Enforcers straight in the eye and telling them where to go," Beatty said. "Come by here to burn down my place. You can see the torches they was going to use laying there in the street. The marshal warned them to forget it, that he wasn't putting up with anything like that —"

"Who is he? Didn't even know we had a marshal."

"Hired on just a bit ago, not even a hour."

"Seen him come riding in, figured he was some hardcase heading for the border. Then when he got with Craig and the others, I wondered maybe —"

Matt slid his forty-five into its holster and faced the crowd. "Like to ask one thing!" he called, and waited until the hubbub had died down. Then, "The bullet that killed Huckaby came from somewhere along the street. If any of you heard the shot or saw the smoke I want to know about it. The killer won't be there now, but it'll give me a place to start from."

"Why bother, Marshal? Whoever it was done us a favor," someone in the crowd said.

"Maybe so," Kollister replied, "but it was still murder, and you can't afford to turn your back on that if you ever want this town to amount to something. So how about it? Any of you hear or see anything, anybody moving around?"

There was murmuring in the still-swelling crowd but no direct answer. It was possible the gunshot had gone unheard and unseen. The killer could have been standing well back inside a room or empty building and fired through an open door or window. With everyone's attention centered on the confrontation at the jail, the actions could easily have passed unnoticed.

Matt started to turn and retreat into his office. The crowd, having now been made aware of all that had taken place by Craig and Beatty, and having had their look at the crumpled bodies of the two dead men, began to press toward him, voicing their congratulations and seeking to shake his hand. He acknowledged them all as best he could, and then paused, catching sight of Seera Ford, her features strained, standing back on the board sidewalk beyond the crush of the crowd, studying him soberly. A fairly well-dressed, elderly man was at her side, and Matt watched as Seera smiled and said something to her companion.

At once Kollister moved toward her, disturbed by the apparent distress the shootings had evoked. It wasn't reasonable for her, a victim of Huckaby ruthlessness, to regret the incident; rather, she should be pleased, or at least relieved, that two of the men who reportedly had a hand in the death of her husband had been brought to account. Further, the fact that the first step in challenging the cattlemen had been made should be encouraging to her. He halted, feeling a hand on his arm. Turning, Matt faced Oren Yates.

"I want to tell you, standing up to that bunch the way you did was really something!" the feedstore man exclaimed. "I was right there in my doorway watching — I seen and heard it all. And shooting that Buck Snapp, don't go feeling bad about it. You didn't have no choice."

Kollister nodded and let his gaze shift to the man's place of business, noting that it was immediately adjoining Beatty's saloon. A wry smile tugged at the corners of his mouth. At least Yates, along with Craig and Hank Beatty, could be ruled out as Travis Huckaby's killer, which boiled it down to the rest of the people living in Shoham.

"Hate killing, same as most folks," he said in reply, "but sometimes a gun's the only answer."

"Except it was a mistake this time," a voice behind him observed. "You're a stranger here, and it could be you don't realize just who's been shot down. One of them's Travis Huckaby — old Hiram's boy."

"I know who they are," Matt said, coming about. The speaker was tall and lean, with deeply lined features.

"We told the marshal all about the Huck-abys, Karl," John Craig broke in, stepping up to Kollister's side. "I reckon he knew what he was doing."

"Did you tell him that Hiram is the biggest man in these parts and that something like this — his son getting killed right here in town — is bound to set him off and bring him and his bunch down on us full blast?"

"You're a mite mixed up, Karl," Craig said. "The marshal didn't shoot Travis. Was somebody hiding —"

"Makes no difference. Hiram'll hold us all responsible. You know how he is same as I do, and we —"

"I'll take care of it," Kollister said. "Happens it's what I've been hired to do."

"Well, you sure best get all primed for it because he'll get his bunch together and come here looking for revenge."

"We'll be lucky if they don't burn the whole town to the ground," another bystander commented. "The more I think about this, the more I figure we're in bad trouble. We should've just let things slide, get along with them best we could."

"Now, that's damn foolishness, Abe, and you know it!" Craig said angrily. "Travis and the men running with him have been

70

getting worse right along!"

The crowd was now gathered closely around Kollister and Craig, along with Beatty, Yates and the man addressed as Karl. Other residents familiar to Matt — Salem, Wheeler, Ferlin Webb and Bert McAdams, the owner of the Bonanza — were also now in evidence.

"Hell, Karl, you know we had to do something!" It was Tom Salem who spoke. His voice was heavy with impatience. "You been saying it right from your pulpit, and now you're back-tracking."

"Maybe so, but I never figured on Travis getting killed. Snapp won't make no difference to Hiram, and neither would any of them others, but his son —"

"Travis's been asking for it," Beatty interrupted.

"That'll make no difference to Hiram," a man standing next to Karl said with a shrug. "The boy was family, and he won't let it pass. Can't afford to."

"Well, I'll tell you one thing for damn sure," another voice stated positively, "I ain't figuring to be around when he comes in after Travis! That old man'll be breathing hell's fire, and anybody he happens to come across is apt to find himself in a bad fix."

Kollister looked across the crowd to where

71

Seera and her elderly friend — probably a transient staying at her hotel — had been standing. They were no longer there, and a quick survey also failed to reveal them. Evidently they had gone back to the Alamo. He'd see her later, talk to her and see what it was that appeared to be troubling her, Matt decided; right now he had something necessary to do.

Shoham was afraid of Hiram Huckaby and what the rancher would do when he came for the body of his son. There was only one answer to that, and that was to head him off: deliver Travis and Snapp to Huckaby before he could get his crew together and ride in. That would eliminate the rancher's reason for coming into town that day, and thus avoid any possible trouble. Then, perhaps after matters had cooled overnight, Hiram Huckaby might take a calmer view of the situation.

"Tom," Kollister said, singling out the livery stable owner, "I'd like to borrow a team and wagon for a bit. Need a tarp or a blanket, too."

Salem nodded, rubbed at his jaw. "Sure, but —"

"Want to load up Travis and Snapp and haul them out to the Huckaby place."

An immediate hush dropped over that

part of the crowd near enough to overhear Matt's words. Several men farther back, thinking they had heard incorrectly, pressed their neighbors for clarification.

"That's what he said, all right. He's taking Travis and Snapp out to the Diamond H!" one explained.

There was a murmur of disbelief. A voice said, "Man's got more guts than a army mule — or else he's dumber'n one."

John Craig considered Matt with a frown. "You sure this is what you want to do, Marshal?"

Kollister nodded. "Best way I can think of to keep the lid on things. It won't be the first time I've delivered a dead man to his people."

"But this here's old Hiram Huckaby's boy —"

"Can't see as that makes any difference," Matt said casually and put his attention on Salem. "I'd like to get started right away. Sure be obliged if you'll get me that rig now."

Salem bobbed and hurried off down the street.

"Might be a good idea if a couple of us went along," Craig said, still not satisfied. "We could sort of help you talk, explain our side of it, back you up."

Kollister gave that thought, "No," he said after a bit. "I want to keep the town out of this as much as I can. Being the marshal, it's up to me to do the explaining."

Suddenly, Matt turned and walked back into his office with no further word. Craig, Beatty and several others followed.

"How do I get to Huckaby's ranch?" he asked, halting beside his desk.

Craig dropped back to the door and pointed up the street. "Go out the same way you came in, but when you get to Marcus's store, take the road forking to your right. It'll lead you to the Diamond H."

There was a rumble of wheels outside and Craig, glancing over his shoulder, added, "Here's Tom with a rig now — must've had one already hitched up for somebody else. I'll have a couple of the boys out there load the bodies for you."

Kollister said, "Fine," and as Craig went through the doorway, Matt crossed to the window and again searched briefly for the sight of Seera Ford. The woman was still not to be seen, but the elderly hotel guest was now standing in the entrance to the Alamo, idly viewing the proceedings in front of the jail.

"How long a drive is it to Huckaby's?" he asked, pivoting slowly.

74

"Take you nigh onto a couple of hours in that rig," Oren Yates answered. "A bit less, maybe."

"Ought to put me back here in time for supper," Matt said, moving for the door. "But if I'm a bit late, don't get all fired up and start looking for me. I'll be back."

Yates grinned and bobbed as he looked about the room. "Yessir, I just bet you will."

# 7

A quarter of an hour later, Matt Kollister was on the road leading northeast out of Shoham and moving steadily for Hiram Huckaby's Diamond H ranch. The midday heat was relentless, and a hush hung over the land as the wild things lay dormant in the sheltering brush while they awaited the cooler hours. Above it all, the sky was a depthless blue with nothing to mar its placid surface but a solitary hawk hunting lazily in a broad circle.

At the crest of a hill Kollister drew the team to a halt. Standing on the seat of the wagon, he had a long look at the country to the north. He could see the main road slicing a fairly straight course across the gray and brown earth, and was relieved to note that no travelers were en route. Such was no real assurance of anything, however, he realized as he took up the lines and put the team back into motion. Fred Larkin could be out there somewhere, just not visible at that particular moment; a prudent man, like the creatures surviving in the area, wisely rested during that time of day. As for himself, Kollister felt he could do nothing but endure the raging temperature. Stopping Hiram Huckaby from riding into Shoham with an armed posse bent on vengeance was of the utmost importance.

The tension of the shoot-out no longer held him in its tight grip, and he once again was at ease. Killing Buck Snapp was to be regretted, just as was the murder of Travis Huckaby; killing a man — any man, be he outlaw or otherwise — was wrong. There had been times since the day he'd first pinned on a star and taken an oath to uphold the law that he had wished he'd chosen some other way of life.

But he hadn't. Like everything else, a man had to take the bad with the good, the disadvantages with the rewards. Still, he'd always wondered — after a shoot-out such as the one he'd just experienced — if there might have been some other way to settle the issue in question, something overlooked in the brittle pressure of the moment, whereby a killing could have been avoided.

Perhaps if he'd talked a bit longer, or listened more, gunfire might have been avoided. But again, as usual, it became apparent that there simply had not been time for such an alternative. Words had been of no avail and a bullet had been the only answer.

Often he was convinced that the star a lawman wore was like a red flag to a ruttish bull, exciting and angering an outlaw and goading him into violence. Larkin had once told him that being a lawman set a man apart, that it isolated him from friends as well as enemies — and even from family sometimes. A kind of resentment seemed to spring up, Larkin claimed, that caused folks he'd known for years to turn away and lawbreakers to declare open season on him. Matt had thought the older man's words a bit farfetched at first, but later, as cynicism pitilessly discolored or destroyed many of his youthful illusions, he had come to agree.

Kollister pushed back his hat and swiped at the sweat on his forehead. His eyes had caught the bright gleam of water a short distance ahead, and he reckoned he was again coming to the other branch of the creek he'd noticed when entering the settlement. Reaching the stream shortly, he cut off the road, avoiding a narrow bridge, and drove the team down to where they could satisfy their thirsts.

As he rested in the cooling shade of cottonwoods growing along the water, Matt gave further thought to the job he'd undertaken. The killing of Travis Huckaby complicated things considerably. He had figured it only a matter of driving the outlaws from Shoham and bringing about an understanding between the cattlemen and the townspeople. Now he was also faced with running down young Huckaby's murderer — and that could be quite a chore. Practically everyone in the settlement could be a suspect since Travis was hated by all.

The horses finished drinking. Taking up the reins, Kollister put the team in motion again, allowing them to ford the creek, which was no more than a foot deep and a half a dozen strides wide at this point.

He was on Huckaby land. That became apparent when he swung the team back onto the road and resumed his course. Cattle were to be seen on the grassy swales and flats to either side, all bearing Huckaby's distinct Diamond H brand. The stock looked fat, and Kollister reckoned that if all of Huckaby's range was as good as this, there was no reason to wonder at the rancher's success.

Kollister drew in slightly, carefully shifted the leathers from right to left hand. Movement in the brush edging the road ahead had caught his attention and sent flags of warning fluttering in his mind. Giving no outward signs of awareness, Matt eased back on the seat and let the fingers of his free hand rest lightly near the gun holstered on his hip. The motion could have been that of some animal — a deer perhaps, or a stray steer — but Kollister had learned long ago never to take anything for granted at such moments.

The team came to an abrupt, sliding halt. Two riders had spurted suddenly from the brush to block the road. Each had a rifle sitting loosely on his saddle horn. Cursing softly, Kollister quieted his team with a firm pull on the lines, still keeping his free hand near his weapon.

"Just where the hell you think you're going?" one of the riders demanded.

Kollister considered the men coldly. Ordinary cowhands working the range for Huckaby, he decided, judging from appearances.

"You know where you are?" asked the second rider, a small, heavily built man. "You're trespassing, mister, and we don't put up with no trespassing here on Diamond H."

Matt shifted on the seat. The change

brought the badge pinned to his shirt into view.

"Hey!" the first cowhand exclaimed. "This here's that tin-star that shot down Buck and got Travis killed!"

The squat man's eyes narrowed. "Expect you're right," he said, and tightened his grip on his rifle. "You got something to say to that?"

"Shot Snapp when he tried to draw on me. I don't know who killed Travis, but I aim to —"

"That ain't how we heard it!" the taller of the pair declared. "We seen Dutch and Ed Waggoner back up a spell, and they was right there. Said you had your deputy bushwhack Travis and then blasted Buck when he jumped you about it."

Matt shook his head. This was the way the incident would be reported to Hiram Huckaby, he guessed. "Nothing to that. It's a lie."

"Well, by God, I'm believing it! Buck and Travis was bunkies of ours, and I reckon we'll just go right ahead and do Mr. Huckaby a good turn and square things up for him and us both," the rider shouted and jacked a cartridge into the chamber of his rifle.

Kollister's right hand moved slightly, and

his pistol came into view. "Forget it," he said in a sharp, warning tone. "I see your trigger finger twitch even a little bit, I'll blow you out of that saddle and load you into the back of this wagon with Travis and Snapp. Goes for both of you."

The rider frowned, glanced at his husky partner and back. "You got them there under that tarp?"

Kollister nodded. "Taking them to Huckaby. Now get out of the way and let me by, or use those rifles. It's too damn hot to sit here and argue."

The two men let their weapons drop; then, under Kollister's unrelenting gaze, they slid them into their saddle boots. That done, the lawman nodded briefly and slapped at the broad backs of his horses with the lines, started them moving forward. He looked at neither of the riders as he drew abreast, allowing his pistol, still in his hand, to speak for him.

When he was a hundred yards or so on up the road, Matt glanced over a shoulder. There was no sign of the pair. They could have gone on about their work, he reasoned, deciding to leave retribution up to Huckaby, or they could have cut off the road and circled around to get in front of him.

A short time later, however, when he

broke out of the brush and trees into a wide clearing and saw the Huckaby place directly before him, he had seen no more of the two cowhands and concluded they had continued on their way.

The ranch house was a long, sloped-roof affair, Kollister noted as he drove under the tall gate with hanging sign that proclaimed the spread as the Diamond H. It was in fine condition, as were the outbuildings — the barns, sheds, crew's quarters, cook-shack and such — which all looked to have just recently been painted or whitewashed.

There was no one in sight, neither around the main house nor in the yard, corrals or structures beyond. A warning again coursed through Kollister as he swung toward the hitchrack; once more his hand strayed to the pistol at his side which only moments earlier he'd restored to its holster.

Curving up to the rack, Matt brought the team to a stop. He could see several horses now, standing in the shadow of a large tree behind the house. One of them was the big chestnut with the silver-trimmed saddle that Travis had been riding. He remembered that both it and Snapp's horse had followed the other Diamond H men when they rode out of town after the shootings.

Kollister had scarcely halted when movement at the sides of the house caught his eye. At each front corner men had appeared; some were holding rifles; others, thumbs hooked in gun belts, appeared ready to use the pistols on their hips.

Matt leaned forward deliberately, and slowly wound the reins about the whipstock; then, settling back, he considered the riders narrowly. Charlie Marshall was among them, as were Ed Waggoner and Dutch Schultz. They were the only ones he recognized.

"Not looking for trouble," he called out. "I'm here to see Huckaby — but if you want to turn it into a chore, then let's get at it. I don't —"

Matt broke off. The front door of the house swung back and a tall, heavily built man with a snow white mustache and beard stepped onto the porch, followed by an attractive young woman.

Arms folded across his broad chest, the man moved to the edge of the porch and halted. He was wearing expensive-looking gray cord pants with the legs tucked into soft black leather boots, a white shirt with pearl buttons and a yellow silk bandanna about his neck. A cowhide vest was open in the front and decorated with silver conchos; a bone-handled pistol was on his hip.

"I'm Huckaby," he said in a hard voice. "Speak up — I'm in a hurry."

Kollister's attention had drifted to the girl. In her early twenties, he guessed, she was a well-developed brown-eyed blonde in corduroy skirt, boots and a red-and-blue-checked shirtwaist. There was an air of arrogant capability about her, and it came to Matt that she was undoubtedly her autocratic father's daughter and took great pride in the fact.

"What's on your mind?" the rancher pressed.

At Huckaby's impatient question, Kollister came back to the business at hand. "I've got your boy and one of your hired hands in the back of this wagon. I'm the marshal at Shoham."

The rancher drew up stiffly, and his jaw hardened as he realized who Matt Kollister was.

"You're the tin-badge that was in on the killing of Travis?"

"I was there," Matt replied evenly. "Had nothing to do with him getting shot."

"Not how it was told to me! You and your deputy ganged up on Travis and Buck and —"

"That's a lie, Huckaby. I don't have a deputy, and while I might have had to kill

85

your son the way he was carrying on, somebody else did it."

Huckaby swung his attention to the men at the left front corner of the house and singled out Marshall. "Charlie, you lie to me?"

The gunman shook his head. "Just told you what Buck said before this jasper cut him down."

"But you don't know if it was true or not?"

Marshall shrugged. "All I know, Mr. Huckaby, is what Buck said."

The rancher stirred, ran fingers through the shock of white covering his head. "You know I don't stand for no lying, Charlie," he stated.

"Wasn't lying," the gunman declared stubbornly. "Only told you what —"

"Never mind," Huckaby broke in, and turned his glance to several men standing beyond the gunman. "Chase, you and Getty come over here and get Travis and carry him into the house. A couple of you others look after Snapp."

The riders named quickly complied, one of them taking a moment to prop the rifle he was holding against the house. Kollister waited in silence, making no effort to assist the men, but keeping his eyes forward on Huckaby and his daughter while the bodies were being removed. When it was done, Matt nodded to the rancher.

"Want to say I'm sorry it happened. I don't hold with killing, and soon as I'm back in town I aim to start hunting down the man who shot your son."

"Ain't no need for that," Huckaby said. "Was my boy, and I take care of my own."

Kollister sighed quietly. Big, rich men were all the same — laws unto themselves. They worried about their names and the fear and prestige they'd built up among others. Nothing could ever be permitted to damage the aura of power and invincibility with which they surrounded themselves and their families, regardless of circumstances.

"No, not this time," Matt said in a flat voice. "I'm the marshal and I'll handle it."

Huckaby's face flushed, and the girl gave him a quick, frowning glance. After a moment, the rancher shook his head.

"How long you been town marshal?"

"Took the job this morning."

"Then I'm going to give you some advice. Showed plenty of brass bringing my boy home to me the way you did, and I like that in a man. But it stops there. Best thing you can do now is hand that star back to John Craig and the rest of that bunch of pussy-footers and ride on before you find yourself in more trouble than you ever saw!"

Kollister smiled humorlessly. "I guess that's the way it's been around here, you holler and somebody jumps."

Huckaby's eyes flashed with anger. He had only to give the word to Charlie Marshall and the others gathered at the corners of the house and they would open up. But Matt was certain Huckaby would not do so; he had earned the rancher's respect and that would stand in his favor — for a while, anyway.

"I run this ranch the way I figure's best — and to suit myself," Huckaby said. "Big as it is, I've got to be tough. If I wasn't, the place wouldn't amount to a damn, and every two-bit rancher and clodhopping hay-shaker in the country would be nipping at my flanks, stealing me blind.

"Can't let down for a minute, not in any way. Same as if I was to let you tend to taking care of Travis's killer. Right away others'd get the idea that I'd gone soft and they could get away with anything they wanted. First thing you know, the Diamond H wouldn't amount to —"

"I know," Kollister said, brushing at the sweat on his face. "I've heard the song before, and it's real sad."

"Then you're admitting I'm in the right?"

"Nope, can't say that I do. I'm agreeing that a man has the right to protect his property, but that doesn't give him leave to walk hard-heeled over everybody just for the sake of keeping them scared."

"You think me taking the boys and going into town after whoever shot Travis — one of them no-account outlaws that's laying around there I figure — is wrong?"

"It is. Town's got a lawman now, and that's something you best remember."

"It's had one before, two or three times, and they never amounted to nothing. Like as not it'll turn out the same, whatever your name is."

"Matt Kollister. I figure to make it different."

"How? Long as them outlaws are hanging around —"

"They won't be much longer. And while we're talking about it, I'm serving notice on you and your crew. When you come to town, come peaceable and behave yourselves, or else you'll answer to me."

Anger again flared in Hiram Huckaby's eyes and colored his face. Beth, too, was showing her irritation.

"You're a mighty big talker," the rancher said.

Kollister's shoulders stirred. "I've been a

lawman for a few years. I've run up against your kind before."

"My kind?" Huckaby echoed mockingly.

"Yes, the kind who figures they own everybody and have got the right to do whatever they please."

"They've got the right because they built themselves up to where they're strong. That's all that counts in this country, Kollister, all that's ever counted — being strong. If a man ain't, he goes down into the dust fast.

"Always been a fight. If it wasn't the Indians trying to beat him down, it was the rustlers or a drought or maybe a blizzard that hit him when he wasn't ready. Sometimes it was even the damn government trying to take his range away from him. Now, if a man can survive all that and still make a life for himself and his family, I figure it's meant for him to do what he has to to keep it. The getting ain't all there is to it in the country, no sir; keeping it is a mighty big chore, too."

Kollister was quiet for a long breath. Then, "I'm not saying you're wrong in wanting to hold on to what you've got, I'm faulting you for the way you go about it. You've got to let the law handle —"

"The hell I do!" Huckaby exploded suddenly. "It never amounted to anything around here, and I don't figure it ever will. And that means nothing's changed. Now, I'm done swapping words with you. We ain't never going to see things in the same light."

"Never thought we would," Matt said coolly, his attention on Beth Huckaby. The girl's mouth was a tight line and her eyes had narrowed with anger. "I want to say it once more: Don't come to town, any of you, unless you're peaceable."

"Expect I'll do as I damn please!" the rancher snapped. "Now, you turn that rig around and get the hell off my land. Won't nobody stop you — you've got my word on that. My daughter here and my boys ain't liking it, but I owe you that much, leastwise till sundown."

Kollister's smile was cynical. "Obliged," he said.

"And something else — you got till noon tomorrow to nab the man that killed Travis. If you ain't done it by then, I'm bringing in my crew to take that town apart board by board till I find him —"

"Don't try it," Kollister cut in coldly. Throwing a glance at the sullen men at the corners of the house, he wheeled the wagon about and started up the lane for the gate.

# 8

Kollister reached the entrance to the yard, passed under the crossbeam of the gate, and turned onto the road that led to Shoham. He was uncertain how firm an understanding he'd established with Huckaby; he'd made his position as the town's marshal clear and served notice that the law would be upheld, but there was little to indicate that the rancher would respect the change.

Nor was he absolutely certain what to expect in the near future. He had originally thought the rancher might bring his men into town that very night, but if his word could be taken, nothing drastic would occur until noon the next day — and then only if Travis Huckaby's murderer had not been caught.

That left it squarely up to him, Matt realized as the wagon clattered along the narrow road. He must find the killer. The hoofs of the horses filled the hot, still air with their soft drumbeat.

Kollister drew out his bandanna and mopped at the sweat on his face and neck. The possibility of a bloody reprisal being visited upon the outlaws, and upon the town, was very real. Ferreting out the killer would be no easy task, for Travis Huckaby had been a man thoroughly hated. There were many who would have wanted to kill him, if all reports on the boy were true, and Matt had had no reason to doubt them.

With not much time to get things done, he'd find Sam Vickers as soon as he reached town and order him to get his bunch together and get out. If they refused, not only would they have to face him, but Hiram Huckaby and his Enforcers as well.

More than likely, some of the Vickers crowd had heeded his first warning, but there would be those old, prideful hardcases such as Vickers himself, Pete Irby, Cherokee Smith and such who took orders from no one and would require driving out. And it would also be necessary to warn the merchants and others living within the bounds of the settlement of the possible danger, should he fail to run down Travis Huckaby's murderer before the deadline.

He'd suggest they barricade their places as much as practical, and stay out of sight once he gave the signal that the rancher and his men were coming. Also, they should have buckets of water and wet sacks handy, as fire would be Huckaby's chief means for bringing the town to terms.

Then, there was the matter of fighting back for those who were so inclined. He'd have to name a meeting place where they could gather, fully armed, at which time he would assign specific positions along the street where they could be the most effective. There was no hope, he felt certain, that Huckaby would not take matters into his own hands once the deadline was reached and —

Matt's thoughts came to a stop. He swore softly. Just beyond a bend in the road, a hundred yards or so ahead, he had seen movement. It was probably the same two cowhands he'd encountered on the way in — this time they might not be so easily turned away.

Matt gave that brief consideration, and then, as the curve in the brush-lined trail provided a dense, ragged wall that hid him from view, he leaned forward, secured the lines around the whip handle so the team would not feel any change, and dropped quickly to the ground.

As the horses continued on down the

road, Kollister stepped into the brush and hurriedly cut diagonally through the undergrowth toward the point where he had seen motion.

A dozen strides later, Matt halted at the sight of a lone horse tied to a small tree. He frowned; if it was the two riders awaiting him in ambush, there should be another horse. Hidden in the depths of a mesquite, Matt searched the area with probing eyes but saw no second animal. Either one of the Diamond H cowhands had gone on, or else he was up against someone different.

Kollister moved on. He could hear the rumbling and rattling of the wagon off to his right. It had now drawn abreast of him in its circuitous route, and shortly would round the curve and be in view of whoever was planning to ambush him.

A flash of color — red and blue — in the brush at the edge of the road again brought Matt to a stop. At that moment, the team broke into sight, plodding stolidly along with the wagon in their wake, and the bit of color rematerialized. Beth Huckaby took a few steps toward the horses, her attention on the empty wagon, and ordered the team to a stop.

Matt, a hard grin splitting his mouth, glided forward silently, stepping in behind the girl just as she realized fully that she had been tricked. Pistol clutched in her hand, she whirled; Kollister caught her around the waist with his left arm while his right hand closed about the weapon she was holding.

"Looking for me?" he asked dryly.

Beth jerked back, began to struggle wildly as she attempted to break free. "Take your hands off me, damn you!" she shouted.

Kollister maintained his vise-like grip. Beth was strong, but her strength was of no avail against his. After a few moments she gave up.

"All right, you've caught me," she said, breathlessly.

Matt wrenched the pistol from her fingers and lowered his arm. Beth stepped away and faced him defiantly.

"Now what?"

He shrugged. "Seems the Huckaby word's not worth much."

"That was his — not mine! If I'd had my way you'd never have left the yard. I don't have to agree with everything he says."

"I figured you did. Way I heard it, old Hiram's word is pure law. Seems I was wrong when it comes to you."

Beth looked away, tugging her skirt back into proper alignment. A wisp of honey-colored hair had come out from beneath the narrow-brimmed man's hat she was wearing and now lay against the creamy texture of her cheek. It occurred to Matt that if she wasn't so hostile and intent on being hard-nosed, Beth Huckaby could be a most appealing woman.

"Pa's gone soft," she said flatly. "I don't hold with letting you off scot-free, but you're the first man I've ever seen stand up to him, I'll give you that. Expect that's why he did it — for all the good it'll do you. You taking me to town and locking me up in your jail?"

"Probably a good idea."

"It's what I'd expect from any lawman the town would hire. Buck the Huckabys, do them dirt — that's all people in Shoham ever have in mind."

"You don't think much of lawmen."

"Not any I've ever come across," Beth shot back. "And if people around here would come to their senses, they'd realize they don't need one. The Diamond H is big enough to look after them if they'd let us. One thing for damn sure, we'd keep those outlaws from taking over."

"And let the likes of your brother have a free hand to do what they please — that what you mean?"

"No, that's not what I mean! Travis was a good-for-nothing. He got what he had coming to him."

"Been told that, too. If he —"

"Travis never did anything in his life but hurt the family, drag the Huckaby name through the mud. He'd been asking for that bullet for a long time — heard Pa tell him that plenty of times!"

"Didn't look like he was grieving much, and you sure don't seem much upset at his death."

Beth brushed at the straying lock of hair. "Why should I be? He might be blood kin but I'm sure not proud of it. I'm glad we're rid of him."

"Then what're you doing here hiding in the brush, waiting to bushwhack me? I figured it was on account of your brother."

"Hell, no!" Beth snapped angrily. "That doesn't mean calf slobber to me — it's what you've done to the family!"

Matt had an idea of what the girl was driving at, but he shook his head. "Makes no sense —"

"Well, it ought to, if you're half as smart as you make out you are. Pa laid it out for you back there at the house: Nobody ever got away before with tromping on Huckaby toes. The Diamond H is — was —"

"King," Kollister supplied.

"Yes, king. And the whole country was afraid to ever cross us. Then you come along, hire out to the town as marshal, and first thing off a Huckaby gets killed."

"Best you keep this straight in your head; I had nothing to do with it other'n being there."

Beth shook her head. Her features were drawn into a deep frown, and the same anger Matt had seen earlier still filled her eyes.

"Makes no damn difference! He was shot while he was talking to you, and three fourths of the people who hear about it will get it wrong and think you did it. Even if you had, it wouldn't mean diddly — those same people would still believe we're letting you get away with it if we don't do something about it.

"Then, even worse, you had the gall to ride into the ranch and tell Pa to his face, in front of all the hired hands, that he's to stay out of hunting down a man who's killed a Huckaby — that it's none of his business!"

Matt smiled humorlessly. "And the way you see it, the family name can't stand that —"

"Can't and won't," Beth corrected.

"Which is what brought you here all

cocked and primed to put a bullet in my back."

"I'm not as charitable as Pa was. Fact is, I was real surprised at him when he didn't have Charlie Marshall and some of the other men shoot you right there in the yard. Probably the reason that he didn't is that you showed more guts than sense.

"But I don't see it that way. You shamed Pa, and you've shamed the Huckaby name — and I don't aim to let you get away with it!"

Matt Kollister studied the girl thoughtfully. "I'm beginning to think you had a pretty smart idea when you talked about me locking you up. Could be the best thing to do till this all blows over."

"It won't be blowing over, not until —"

"But I'm thinking something else now," Kollister continued. "We just might do some trading — forget about jail, if you'll do me a favor."

Beth stiffened and her eyes narrowed. "If you think you're talking to one of those husseys down at Dolly's Place and that I'll buy my way —"

Matt brushed at the sweat on his face. "Not what I had in mind. If I was looking for a woman for that, I'd sure not pick a hell-cat like you," he said.

Beth's expression turned from one of angry outrage to confusion that bordered on embarrassment.

"Then — what —"

"I'm a stranger here, you know that. I've had a feeling I'm not getting both sides of the story when it comes to the town and the ranchers. I'd like to hear what you've got to say about it."

Beth was silent for a few moments, her attention on Kollister as he rodded the cartridges from the pistol he had taken from her and tossed them off into the brush.

"Don't know what I can tell you that you don't already know," she said.

"About all that amounts to is that there's trouble between the cattlemen and the town," Matt replied, handing the weapon back to her. "I'm told your pa wants to run things and —"

"That's not the way it is — not exactly," the girl cut in quickly, and pointed to a nearby tree. "Let's get over there in the shade. We can talk better there."

Without waiting for Kollister to agree, she turned and crossed the short distance to where a small acacia laid a patch of shadow upon the baked soil. Gathering her skirt beneath her, she sat down on a hummock of dead grass and motioned Matt to a log close by.

"It's not who's going to run the town that's the problem," she said as Kollister settled himself. "It's what goes on there."

"Meaning?"

"Well, we never had any trouble to speak of until that bunch of outlaws started hanging around. Truth is, we didn't give them much thought. The town was always a sort of overnight stop for their kind riding for the border, and since they were just passing through, they were usually no problem. Then this bunch that's there now showed up, and Craig talked them into staying."

"According to what I was told, they never caused any trouble — up till now. Merchants claim that they behaved themselves because they wanted to keep on good terms —"

"Maybe with the folks in town, but that's sure not true for the rest of us!" Beth declared.

"They give you ranchers trouble?"

"Plenty, and not only the ranchers but the sodbusters and pilgrims, too."

Kollister made no reply. Such verified his belief that Vickers and his outlaw followers had in no way changed their lives. In the beginning they may have kept hands off the merchants and residents of Shoham while they confined their lawless activities to the surrounding area, but that was no longer the fact. If he had solid proof, he'd have reason to jail them and thus make his job simpler.

"Craig and the rest of the town think that bunch is so lily-white! Truth is, there's been rustling and holdups, and several women caught out alone bothered."

"I believe it," Matt said, "and with a little proof I could jug the lot of them. I know Vickers from long back."

Beth was staring at him closely, seemingly surprised at his words. "I'll remember that. Pa's not so much interested in taking over the town as he is in getting rid of those outlaws."

Kollister touched the star on his shirt pocket. "Tell him he can forget that. The law will take care of them."

"The law — meaning you?"

"Meaning me. The town's realized they made a mistake letting Vickers and the others hole up there. They hired me to get rid of them, along with making peace between the ranchers and the folks in Shoham. I want you to tell that to your pa."

"This the truth — on the level?" Beth asked in a doubting voice. "I'm finding it hard to believe that Craig and the others've changed their thinking, and Pa'll look at it the same way."

"Take my word for it — they have. I can do the job if he'll stay out of it. That means forgetting that noon tomorrow deadline he set for me to find your brother's killer. Maybe I can turn up the man by then, and maybe I can't. It's not all that easy."

"Why not? It's bound to be one of those outlaws."

"Can't bank on that, not if Travis had as many enemies as I've been told he had."

Beth shrugged. "He had plenty, that's for sure. I'll talk to Pa, see if I can get him to hold off and give you a chance — but I'm not making any promise. Him holding off until tomorrow noon was a surprise. What I said about those outlaws, if you want any proof of what they've done I can take you —"

"Later," Kollister said, getting to his feet. The day was growing old and he'd accomplished what he'd hoped to do — for the time being — enlist Beth's aid in trying to buy himself more time where Hiram Huckaby was concerned. "Just had to be sure in my mind that what I figured was true. I'm obliged to you, and we'll both forget about you and the ambush."

Beth had come erect. "That's right nice of you," she said dryly, turning toward her horse. "Now, if I find out all you've told me is just so much sheep-dip, that you've tricked me, I'll be waiting for you somewhere again — and next time you won't take me by surprise."

"You just talk to your pa. Keep him out of my way, and things'll work out fine."

"Maybe," the girl said. Then, yanking the reins of her horse loose, she swung up into the saddle and rode off.

It was near six o'clock when Matt reached the edge of Shoham and turned into its dusty street. Levi Marcus was standing in front of The Emporium, and farther down a solitary rider was coming to a stop at the Bonanza's hitchrack. Other than those two, there was no one in sight and the town looked deserted at that near-supper hour.

Kollister drove direct to Salem's Livery Barn at the opposite end of the street and wheeled the wagon through the wide, open doorway into the shadowy interior of the sprawling building. The roustabout who did odd jobs around the place advised Kollister that Tom Salem was not there.

"Tell Salem I'm obliged," Matt said as he

came off the seat. "I'll settle up with him later."

The hostler, one hand holding on to the bridle of a horse, the other thrust deep into a pocket of his overalls, nodded.

"Sure, I'll tell him."

Kollister wheeled, cut back to the street and turned right for his office.

The town no longer gave the impression of having been abandoned. Hurrying toward him now were Bert McAdams, John Craig, Webb, Yates and several other townspeople, all summoned hastily from whatever they had been doing at the sight of him driving down the street. Before he could reach the door to his office, they were upon him.

"How'd you make out?" Craig asked immediately. His hurried effort had brought small wet patches of sweat to his face, and he was breathing hard. "We was sort of worrying, you being gone so long. You have any trouble?"

"Some. Nothing serious," Matt replied, leaning up against the wall of the building.

"Then you saw Huckaby," McAdams said.

"Got there just in time to head him off. He's got it in his head that one of the Vickers bunch shot Travis. Gave me till noon tomorrow to catch whoever it is, or else he's taking matters into his own hands."

"That means he'll be bringing them gunfighters of his to town and —"

"Says he's going to find the man who did it if he has to take the place apart board by board. Could be he'll hold off a bit, however — had a talk with his daughter after I left the ranch, and she's going to see if she can get him to give me more time."

"You believe her?" Craig asked, frowning.

"Expect her word's as good as anybody's," Matt said. He had not mentioned the girl's attempt to ambush him, nor did he intend to. It would serve no good purpose, and if he was to succeed in healing the breach that lay between the town and the ranchers, such incidents were best forgotten.

Ferlin Webb shook his head. "I don't know. Always had her figured for being just as ornery as the old man."

"Huckaby seemed a fair man to me," Kollister said. "He's got all the faults that come with getting big and powerful, but he listened to me."

"That's something," Craig agreed. "Don't think anybody from here's ever got him to do that before. You got any plans for stopping him, just in case you don't find that killer?"

"Expect we'd best get set for him, in case the girl can't get him to hold off and I don't come up with the man who shot Travis," Kollister replied, and outlined the measures he felt the people of the town should take to protect themselves and their property — concluding with the suggestion that any who wished to side him with guns should meet him there at the jail when a signal was given warning of the rancher's approach.

"I take it you ain't got much faith in Huckaby not coming," Oren Yates said morosely.

Matt shrugged. "Best to play it safe."

"You got any idea who it was that shot Travis?" Webb wondered. "Could nip this thing in the bud if you could lay him by the heels and have him locked up and waiting for the judge."

"Nope, not the slightest. Aim to get started on that right away, soon as I hunt up Vickers and have a few words with him."

"Words?" Craig echoed, glancing about.

"The kind that'll send him and his bunch on their way. They're what's sticking in the craws of the ranchers. All the time you were letting them hang around here, thinking they were just loafing and behaving themselves, they were out rustling cattle and holding up pilgrims and the like. We get shut of them, it'll be a big step towards patching up this feud between you folks and the cattlemen."

"You tell them you'd been hired to do just that — run the outlaws out?" Craig asked anxiously.

"They know it," Matt assured him, "but I —"

"What if one of them's the one that killed Travis?" Yates wanted to know. "Won't running them off rile old Hiram, make him think we don't care whether he catches the man or not?"

"Hard to tell how he'll take it, but I'm not worrying about that. I've got to do what I figure's best for the town," Kollister replied, and stepped up into his office. "Anyway, it'll be me he'll blame. Fact is, he's laying the whole thing on my back."

"Just how he'd look at it, all right," Yates said.

The half dozen or so persons who had hurriedly collected in front of the jail with Craig and the other merchants now began to drift away, stating they had best get back to their respective businesses.

"Going to leave it up to you men to get things ready for tomorrow," Matt said to Craig and Yates when they were alone. "I'd handle it myself, but there's something I best do right away. After that's done I'm going to grab myself a bite of supper and then start asking questions around town to see if I can learn anything about the killer."

"That something you mentioned — does it have to do with Vickers and his bunch?" Craig asked.

"It does. I want them gone by morning."

"Well, I'll save you a little time," the merchant said. "I think most of them's over at the Trail's End."

"Trail's End? I thought it was the bar in the Palace Hotel they hung around."

"Ain't no gambling goes on there. When they're wanting to play chuck-a-luck or faro or the like, they go to the Trail's End."

Kollister nodded. "Then that's where I'll be going." Pivoting, he left his office and returned to the street.

# 9

The early evening had brought no break in the heat, and when Kollister stepped back out into the sunlight, he immediately crossed to the opposite flank of the street where he would have the benefit of the shade cast by buildings lining its west side.

As he passed in front of the Alamo Hotel, he glanced into its darkened lobby but saw no one. Nor was there anyone visible through the window of the adjoining restaurant. Seera Ford, he guessed, was probably in her kitchen making preparations for the evening meal. He could use a good supper — the last food he'd eaten had been that morning on the trail — but somehow the need for a meal had become less important to him than seeing Seera Ford again.

That realization puzzled Matt. He had never taken any serious interest in a woman, being forever preoccupied with the task of being a lawman, but now a change had come about. Although they were barely acquainted, he was finding Seera's image constantly in his mind, poised there like a soft shadow studying him with her cool, blue eyes while she favored him with that calm, almost sad smile.

"Marshal —"

Kollister hesitated at the interruption; it was Ferlin Webb. Matt had drawn abreast of the gun shop, and its owner was standing in the doorway, a canvas apron covering the front of him. A disassembled pistol he was working on was in his hands.

"Just wanted you to know that tomorrow I'll be proud to side you if you need be. Got plenty of guns and ammunition, too, and anybody else feeling the same and wanting to borrow a weapon's welcome to help themselves."

Matt smiled, nodded. "Obliged. Just hoping it won't come down to that," he said, and continued on his way.

The Trail's End was immediately ahead. As was customary with him at such moments, Kollister drew his forty-five and checked its action and loads. He found both to his satisfaction and sliding the pistol back into its oiled holster, he angled up to the doorway of the saloon and entered.

Halting just within, Kollister made a swift

appraisal of the establishment: a bar extending across its far wall, a piano nearby, tables scattered about with a cleared space in the center for dancing, gambling equipment along the left side, and a back door in the rear right-hand corner. Smoke hung thick about the lamp chandeliers suspended by ropes from the ceiling, and the smell of whiskey, tobacco and coal oil was strong.

Although there were few patrons in evidence at that hour, two men stood behind the bar, one of whom Matt recognized as Simon Deal, the owner. Dealers idle at the gaming tables and several gaudily clad women were sitting around chatting animatedly, all ready and waiting for the night's business to begin.

Kollister had nothing more than a passing, self-protective interest in these people, however, his attention finally halting and centering on a group of men lounging at a table directly in front of the bar. Immediately the lawman moved toward them, ticking off their identities in his mind as he did: Vickers, Pete Irby, Calico Hays, Billy Blue and Cherokee Smith. The Mexican *vaquero,* Copio Benavidez, was not present, nor was the stranger he'd seen with them earlier that day. Perhaps they and some of those he had not yet encountered had heeded his warning and ridden on. If true, his job would be a bit easier.

Silence dropped suddenly over the house as Kollister, walking with deliberate slowness, approached the counter. Simon Deal nodded, and Vickers, one arm resting on the back of his chair, grinned.

"Howdy there, Marshal," he greeted. As Matt circled the table and came to a halt in front of it, facing him and his friends, Vickers added, "Boys, we got us some real important company — the law!"

"Danged if we ain't!" Irby declared. "How about a drink, Marshal?"

Kollister coldly ignored the invitation. Touching each of the outlaws with a narrowed glance, he fixed his eyes on Vickers.

"Warned you this morning that I wanted you and your bunch out of town. Expected you to be gone by now."

Sam Vickers threw the butt of the cigar he was smoking at a cuspidor and shook his head. "We just ain't took the notion yet, have we, boys?"

There was a murmur of agreement. Calico Hays brushed his hat to the back of his head. "And far as I know we ain't about to either," he said.

"We sort of like it here," Irby added. "We just don't see no reason to move."

114

"I can give you a couple," Kollister said, folding his arms across his chest and leaning back against the bar. "Besides what you're pulling here in town, you've been rustling cattle and holding up folks traveling through."

"Who the hell says so?" Vickers demanded, coming up a bit straighter in his chair.

"I've got the proof," Matt replied, "and the whole bunch of you are mighty close to getting strung up. On top of that, one of you shot and killed a man out there on the street this morning — son of one of the ranchers. I see the *vaquero's* not here. He the one that did it and's already took out?"

"He's gone, all right," Vickers said, "but it sure wasn't him that plugged that jasper."

"Was one of you, then?"

Vickers laughed. "You're doing some fishing, Marshal, and you're wasting your time. Maybe it was one of us and maybe it wasn't, but you sure ain't never going to find out from me."

"I reckon it don't matter much," Kollister said indifferently. "I'm looking for the ranchers to hit town tomorrow all set to clean you out. The menfolk of some of those women you bothered are wanting blood, and the rest of them will be bringing ropes all aiming to put a stop to the rustling that's been going on around here. If it was one of you that killed young Huckaby, you'll be dead before dark, anyway."

Vickers was silent for a long minute. Then he said, "You expecting me to swallow that hogwash?"

"I'm saying you'd better. I just got back from the Huckaby ranch and I know what they're thinking. But I'm not letting it go that far. I'm damned if I'm going to let you and your bunch be the cause of my town getting shot up."

Vickers drew a fresh cigar from the leather case in his vest pocket, bit off the closed end and spat the tip onto the floor.

"Meaning?" he said as he thumbnailed a match into flame and lit the weed.

"I want you all out of here by morning," the lawman said flatly. "I want you gone — and you're to stay gone."

The tension in the saloon abruptly became as thick as the clouds of smoke clinging to the ceiling. Irby shifted on his chair, and Cherokee Smith took up his glass and downed the last few drops of whiskey that it contained. The kid, Billy Blue, shook his head angrily.

"Hell! No lousy coyote tin-badge is going

to tell me what I got to do," he declared. "I'm —"

The young outlaw never got to finish what he intended to say. Matt Kollister, as smooth and fast as a striking rattlesnake, drew his pistol, took a long step forward and clubbed Blue solidly on the side of the head. Billy went out of his chair sideways and down onto the floor in a quivering heap.

Gun still in hand, Kollister stepped back. His features were a cold, expressionless mask dominated by narrowed, colorless eyes.

"Anybody else want to say something?" he asked softly.

There was no reply. Vickers puffed steadily on his cigar and Cherokee toyed with his empty glass while Irby and Hays sat motionless, staring down at Billy Blue's unmoving shape.

The lawman nodded. "I take it then that I'm understood. You'll all be out of town by morning. If I run across any of you when I make my early rounds, don't bother to talk. Just go for your gun because I aim to kill you."

Without turning his head, he added, "Bartender, that back door unlocked?"

It was Simon Deal who answered. "Yessir, it sure is."

Continuing to hold the pistol cocked and ready in front of him, Kollister began to back toward the corner of the saloon and the exit there. Halfway to it, he paused.

"Want to say that if any of you make a move to draw iron or try following me, I won't wait for morning."

Resuming his slow retreat, Matt came to the door. The knob turned in his hand, and the panel swung inward. Stepping quickly through the opening, the lawman pulled the door closed and hurriedly crossed behind the saloon to its adjacent neighbor, Ferlin's Gun & Saddle Shop. There, stepping in behind a pile of empty boxes and other trash, Matt waited.

When a full five minutes had passed and no one had emerged from the rear of the Trail's End or appeared in what he could see of the street fronting it, Kollister decided the outlaws had taken him at his word. Holstering his pistol, he headed along the backs of the buildings for the Alamo Hotel. When he reached the passageway that lay between the hostelry and Webb's, he turned into it and made his way to the street.

Kollister came to a stop, suspicion lifting within him. Two riders had come in from the north end of town and were heading, it appeared, for the Palace. They had the look of trouble — and both were vaguely familiar.

# 10

He was right, Matt saw as he stepped out into the street and strode toward the riders — he knew them. They were the two Diamond H men who had stopped him that morning when he was crossing Huckaby range on the way to the ranch. They had threatened to take matters into their own hands then, and it could be they had ideas along the same line now.

"Marshal —"

Matt glanced to his right. John Craig had come out onto the landing fronting his general store. Standing beside him was Seth Wheeler. Evidently the merchant had had intentions of telling him something, but Craig saw the Diamond H men at the same moment that he called, and now fell silent, sensing trouble.

A few others had come out into the open, and were either waiting and watching from the vantage point of their businesses or had paused on the sidewalk. Matt let his eyes sweep farther along the street, making certain that no surprises were taking shape behind or to either side of him. There appeared to be no threat.

He saw Seera Ford in that brief diversion. She was standing on the porch of the hotel, her attention centered on him. But there was no time to acknowledge her presence; the two cowhands were definitely heading for the Palace Hotel and its bar.

"Hold it!" he yelled to the men, lengthening his stride.

Both riders pulled to a stop, lazily turned to face him.

"Yeh?" the heavy-set one drawled. "Something eating on you, Marshal?"

"Not exactly the right time of day for you to be visiting a saloon," Matt said, squaring himself in front of the pair. The hush along the street had deepened, and the only sound was a lone quail somewhere beyond The Emporium, calling plaintively into the evening. "There a reason?"

"Well, now, maybe there is and maybe there ain't," the taller and younger of the two replied. "Anyways, since when did they pass a law saying fellows like Jake and me have to come in at some special time for a swallow of red-eye?"

"No law like that far as I know," Matt said coolly, folding his arms across his chest, "but working cowhands are usually still on the range about now."

"Do tell," the man called Jake said. "What about that, Otto? This here marshal's real smart. He knows more about our jobs than we do!"

Otto shrugged. "He just thinks he does. I figure he ain't near as smart as he figures."

The pair were looking for trouble, that was certain, Kollister decided. He wondered if Hiram Huckaby had sent them in to deliberately provoke an incident — or could it be the work of Beth Huckaby? He doubted Hiram would break his word, but about the daughter Matt wasn't too sure.

"Truth is, Mister Lawman," Jake said, swiping at the sweat shining on his leathery face, "the boss turned us loose. They're planting Travis and poor old Buck this evening — thanks to you — and nobody's doing any work. That shorten up your nose some?"

"Answers my question," Matt said evenly.

"Then you ain't complaining none if we go right ahead and have us a couple of drinks and do some card playing?"

"Nothing to me, but the way you talked this morning sounded like you were plenty close friends of Travis and Snapp. Makes me wonder why you aren't back there at the ranch for the burying service."

"Ain't nothing we can do for them there —"

"But there is here, that it?" the lawman cut in. "You come looking for trouble?"

"Now hold on, Marshal!" Jake said. "We ain't —"

"Huckaby send you in to stir things up — or was it Beth?"

"No, sir!" Otto declared. "Nothing like that. We ain't even talked to them today."

Kollister studied the pair closely. They could be telling the truth; Huckaby could have suspended work while he buried Snapp and his son. Such was common practice.

"Is it all right if we get going now?" Jake asked in a hopeful voice. "Me and Otto's drier'n last year's cotton, and we sure would like to get ourselves a drink."

A thought occurred to Kollister. "You headed for the bar in the Palace?"

"Was where we was going —"

"Seems I was told you Diamond H boys did your drinking in the other saloons. Why'd you change?"

Jake slanted a glance at his younger companion; again he brushed at the sweat on his face. "I sure can't answer that, Marshal, 'cause I don't know why. Just kind of got stuck in our minds, I reckon. It make a difference to you?"

Kollister shook his head. The Palace was the usual hangout of Vickers and his crowd, and it was possible Jake and Otto had planned to go there for a definite reason. But the outlaws, at least the principal ones, were in the Trail's End at the moment, and like as not they would stay there for the remainder of the evening.

"Palace is fine with me. Main thing I want you to get straight is that I won't allow any hell raising. Get out of line and I'll lock you up."

Otto rubbed at his jaw. "Ain't never been a Diamond H man locked up in your jail, Marshal. Mr. Huckaby just won't stand for it."

"There's always a first time," Kollister said and pivoting, started back down the street.

"And it sure could be the last time, too," Matt heard Otto reply as he and Jake continued on for the Palace.

He was not fully satisfied with what he'd been told. As he walked purposefully along, steps pointed for the Alamo Hotel and a meal in Seera Ford's restaurant, the hunch that Otto and Jake were not as innocent as they professed grew stronger.

"Marshal — you got a minute?"

It was John Craig again. Wheeler was no longer with him, and most of the bystanders and onlookers he'd noted a bit earlier were gone. Halting, Kollister waited for the merchant to join him in the center of the street.

"Sure."

"Seen you talking to them two Huckaby riders. You figure they're up to something?" Craig asked.

"Was wondering about that, yeh."

"Come to me old Hiram could have sent them, aiming to tie you up somehow so's he and the rest of his bunch could ride in —"

"Gave me his word he'd wait until noon tomorrow," Kollister cut in, frowning. "I think he'll stand by it."

Craig looked off toward the north, and the road down which the rancher would come. "Maybe," he said in a doubtful voice. "But I ain't putting much stock in any of the Huckabys. Heard about that little fracas you had in the Trail's End —"

"News travels fast," Kollister murmured dryly.

"It was Wheeler. He'd gone over to get himself a drink. Got to the door and seen you there, talking. Said you gave Vickers and them orders to be out of town by morning, and when that smart-alecky Billy Blue give you some sass, you buffaloed him good."

"About the size of it."

"You think they'll do what you told them to?"

The lawman shrugged. Seera Ford was standing on the porch of the hotel. She appeared to be waiting for him. "Vickers's kind don't take kindly to being ordered around. Usually need a gun to persuade them."

"Then why'd you go to the trouble of talking to them?"

"Always figure a man's entitled to a fair warning before he faces up to dying. Sometimes it works and they ride on without any argument."

"Sure like to think Vickers and his crowd'd do that, but I kind of got my doubts."

"Probably right," Kollister said. "I'm a mite hungry and if you —"

"Still thinking some about Jake Harmon and Otto Lewis — they're the two you was just talking to. I got a bad feeling about them. Sure wouldn't put it past Huckaby to —"

"Forget about it," Kollister said, gaze still on Seera Ford. "Soon as I get myself a bite of supper I'll drop back by the Palace. I aim to keep an eye on them."

"Glad to hear that," Craig said, turning away as the lawman moved off. The merchant halted. "I've got things pretty well set for tomorrow. Like to sort of go over the plan —"

"I'll see you later about it," Matt said, and continued on his way.

Seera was standing just inside the door of the hotel as he entered. A soft smile of welcome was on her lips.

"I saw you drive in," she said as he paused beside her.

There was a note of relief in her voice. He looked at her closely. "That mean you worried some about me?"

Her shoulders stirred. "I guess I did."

Matt glanced about the lobby. There was no one there, but shifting his attention to the adjoining restaurant, visible through the connecting doorway, he saw the elderly man he'd noticed with her that morning sitting at a table having his evening meal.

"No need to fret about me," Kollister said. "You know what they say about old relatives and bad pennies — they always turn up."

Seera laughed. "I'm never sure about the pennies. Expect you'd like some supper."

"I'm hungry enough to eat leather."

She pressed a key into his hand. "Your room's all ready, Number Five. Go along and wash up. I'll have everything waiting by the time you're back."

Matt let his fingers linger briefly about hers; then, as she looked at him questioningly, he released his grip and headed off down the hall. It had been a sudden impulse, and he wasn't sure himself just what his meaning had been. But he did know that he was greatly attracted to Seera Ford, and perhaps the pressure of her slender hand was a subconscious way of showing it.

He reached his room and found it locked. Inserting the key, he opened the door and stepped inside, finding his quarters pleasant although somewhat dark and filled with trapped heat. Stepping to the window in the opposite wall, he raised the sash. At once he felt the touch of fresh, cooler air.

Coming about, he crossed to the bed where his gear had been deposited. There was a clean shirt inside his blanket roll, Matt recalled. He moved next to the washstand, finding the china pitcher full. Pouring a quantity of the tepid water into the companion bowl, he washed himself down, making good use of the soap and cloth Seera had provided.

That done, feeling less weary, Kollister

dressed. After considering and putting aside the thought of shaving, he returned to the lobby. It was still deserted, a fact that attested to the dearth of guests. Passing on through into the restaurant, he halted just within its portiered entrance. The elderly transient was yet at his table, and as Seera hurried up from the rear of the room she noticed the lawman's attention on the man.

"Oh, I don't think you two've met," she said, motioning Matt toward the solitary diner. "Marshal Kollister, this is Mr. Henry Bell. He's staying here at the hotel."

Bell, raising himself slightly in his chair, extended a hand to Matt. "A real pleasure," he said in a low voice.

Kollister accepted the greeting and, from habit, gave the man a swift scrutiny. Probably in his mid-fifties, he had white hair and a sharply contrasting black mustache and beard. His eyes were small, set close together, and a sort of faded brown. A black string tie closed the collar of his white shirt and he was wearing what appeared to be an almost new pearl gray business suit.

"The pleasure's mine," Matt said. Then, nodding, he followed Seera to the back of the room.

She paused by a table set for two and motioned him to be seated. Stepping to the door leading into the kitchen, she said something to someone beyond his view, then turned and came back. He rose in polite deference, and she settled in the chair opposite.

"I decided to wait and eat with you," she said.

He smiled. "I appreciate that. Nothing like a pretty woman to fire up a man's appetite."

His show of gallantry surprised him, but again, there was something about Seera Ford that stirred and awakened a boldness within him.

At that moment the elderly waitress appeared, carrying a tray upon which there were two plates; one was well covered with steaming food, the other piled with hot biscuits and a mound of fresh butter. There was also a pot of coffee to be poured into the cups already on the table.

"I know you're hungry so go ahead and eat," Seera said as the waitress moved off. "We can talk later. I want to know what all happened when you got to Huckaby's. I haven't had a chance to talk to John Craig or any of the others yet. What was that all about down there in front of the Trail's End a bit ago?"

Kollister grinned. "I reckon there's something to this about a woman's curiosity after all," he said, and set to work on his meal of steak, potatoes, gravy and greens. He was even hungrier than he'd thought. When he'd finished he found Seera, her plate only half empty, smiling at him.

"Does my heart good to see a man eat and enjoy his meal."

"Hard not to enjoy grub like that," Matt replied, refilling his coffee cup from the enamel pot. "You've got a good cook."

"Thank you, but that's my job. We don't do enough business anymore to pay someone. Clara — she's the woman who just brought our meal in — and I sort of share the work."

"Then it hasn't always been this way — slow, I mean."

"No, there was a time when the ranchers and the homesteaders would come in on the weekends and do their buying. Most of them would eat here and there'd always be a few who'd stay overnight and go to church next day. And there was always people traveling through going north to Denver or east to Texas and the like. We don't see any of that anymore, or the stagecoach either. The company changed the route so that it missed us after things got so bad."

"I see."

"We had the outlaws hanging around,"

Seera continued in her low, quiet way, "and the Huckabys — Travis mostly, and the crowd that ran with him — riding in and doing a lot of shooting and hoorawing. Between the two bunches, it was pretty miserable and dangerous for everybody."

"But not together. I was told they seemed to avoid having anything to do with each other."

"I guess that's right. At first the outlaws were no bother, at least to us in town; it was all Travis and his friends. Then Vickers and his crowd — there's about a dozen of them — just sort of took over —"

"You say there was a dozen in the bunch?" Matt cut in. "Didn't realize there were that many who —"

Kollister paused, attention on Henry Bell, who had finished his meal and was getting to his feet. Turning his head, the elderly man acknowledged Seera and Kollister with his glance, nodded and disappeared into the hotel lobby.

"What do you know about him?" Matt asked. "He a regular customer here?"

Seera frowned. "No, he's been here about ten days or so now."

"He ever say why he came here? Doesn't have the looks of a rancher or a slicked-up gambler, and he carries his gun in a shoulder holster. My guess would be that he's an eastern businessman."

"You're right," said Seera. "Told me one time that he liked Shoham and was hunting around for something to invest in. Why are you curious about him?"

Kollister shrugged, grinned. "The lawman in me, I guess — always wonder about a stranger. Goes with the job."

"But everybody is a stranger to you here, except maybe some of those outlaws."

Matt glanced toward the street. It was almost full dark, and lamps in the windows of the stores were being lit.

"You got me there," he said. "Sure can't go digging into everybody in town. There is one I'd like to know more about, however, and that I aim to question."

Seera frowned. "Who?"

Matt considered the woman gravely. "You. Never had any woman take hold of me like you have."

Seera colored slightly. "You're tired, and you were hungry; it'll pass. Now tell me what happened out at Huckaby's. Did you have much trouble with him?"

"Not much. He's hard, but I figure him for an honest man and one who'll keep his word. Gave me until noon tomorrow to find the man who killed Travis. Says he'll bring his men and do it himself if I don't. He thinks it was one of the Vickers bunch."

"Do you?"

Kollister shook his head. "Doesn't jibe. Way I see it, if one of them wanted to kill Travis, he wouldn't bother to take a potshot at him from cover. Figuring the kind of jasper Travis was — hated by just about everybody in these parts — the killer'd call his hand right out in the open and do his shooting. Why go to the trouble of bush-whacking a man when people will give you a vote of thanks for sending him to the bone-yard?"

Seera nodded. "Makes sense. Did you see Huckaby's daughter — Beth?"

"She was right there with him, and then I ran into her later, on my way back." Again Matt omitted mention of the ambush Beth Huckaby had planned for him. "Said she'd do what she could to keep her pa calmed down."

"I don't know her very well anymore," Seera said, studying her empty cup. "She's real pretty, isn't she?"

"Never gave it much thought," Kollister replied. "Struck me as being more of a son than a daughter to Huckaby."

"I think that's how she always felt about herself, Travis being the way he was."

"Well, I'm hoping she can talk Huckaby into holding off a bit longer'n noon tomorrow before he —"

"Marshal! Marshal!"

The shout came from the street. Kollister lunged to his feet and rushed to the hotel's porch. A man was hurrying up through the half-dark from the direction of the Trail's End, evidently heading for the jail where he expected to find the lawman. Then he saw Matt, and immediately veered toward him.

"Marshal — best you come quick! Pete Irby's gone and shot Jake Harmon! The way it's looking, he's going to kill Otto Lewis, too!"

# 11

Matt came off the Alamo's porch in a long stride. Clapping a hand against the pistol on his hip to keep it from jarring out of its low-cut holster, he started toward the Trail's End Saloon. So they hadn't gone to the Palace after all!

The man who had come for him, a small, wiry cowhand with pants tucked Texas style into his scarred boots, ranged in alongside him.

"You sure better watch it, Marshal! That bunch in there's plumb ugly!"

Kollister, without slackening his pace, hurried on. Oren Yates had come out in front of his store; just emerging from the Bullhead Saloon and moving to join him was Hank Beatty. There were several other persons along the shadowed way as well, drawn into the open by the shouts of the cowhand or the sound of the gunshot. Some watched him rush by in silence, others called out questions.

The lawman was oblivious to all. His mind was centered on the problem that waited for him at the Trail's End. He needed no warning as to the danger he would encounter when he entered Simon Deal's saloon; at such soaring moments of violence there was always a risk. A man gripped by crushing tension, a gun in his hand — only too often the slightest provocation caused him to kill again.

Kollister reached the front of the Trail's End. A half dozen men had gathered about the saloon's entrance, and as Matt approached, Ferlin Webb came forward to meet him.

"It's the Vickers bunch — they're all drunk. Be careful, Marshal," he said.

Matt nodded, drew his pistol and moved through the doorway. The faint acrid odor of burnt gunpowder still hung in the warm air, and the saloon lay in silence. Without hesitation Kollister drew to one side where he would have a solid wall to his back and thus avoid silhouetting himself against the night.

There were a dozen or so men and several of the saloon's women present. Harmon lay sprawled in front of the counter, gun still clutched in his hand. His partner, Otto

Lewis, was sitting at a nearby table, half out of his chair as if he intended to lunge to his feet and either go for his pistol or make a run for the door.

Pete Irby, hat pushed to the back of his head, features flushed from liquor, lounged against the bar, heel of his left boot hooked carelessly over the brass rail. At a table close by, Sam Vickers sat with two of the outlaw crowd that Kollister had not met. Also with him was the kid, Billy Blue — the left side of his face swollen and discolored. All looked on in dry amusement.

"Put that gun away, Irby," Matt ordered in a hard, no-quarter voice. No other drawn guns were in sight among the outlaws.

Irby grinned, slid the weapon back into its holster. At once Otto Lewis lurched to his feet. His jaw was set, and his eyes were wide and filled with anger and hate. Matt waved the man back.

"Forget it!" he snapped. Crossing to the bar, he knelt beside Harmon and felt for a pulse.

"He's plenty dead," someone along the counter said. "Pete got him good."

Kollister drew himself erect. He looked beyond the smirking Irby to Simon Deal, still behind his bar. As with most all of Shoham's merchants, he knew little about the man, could only judge from a first impression. Deal had struck him as being as straight as could be expected.

"You want to tell me what happened here?" asked Matt.

Deal came out from behind the counter and paused at its end. He wore the pants and vest of a faded brown suit, but no coat; no necktie graced the closed collar of his white shirt.

"Got to say it was a fair fight," the saloon man said with a shrug. "Jake and Otto came in here not long after you left, started jawing at Pete. Then next thing I knew, Jake hollered for Pete to go for his gun and then went for his own. Pete was faster."

Kollister considered that for several moments, then turned his attention to Otto Lewis. "That the way you saw it?"

Lewis stirred nervously on his chair for a brief time, head down, and then nodded. "Yeh, reckon so — but everybody knows Jake weren't no match for Pete."

"Then he sure'n hell hadn't ought to've called out Pete," Vickers observed, finishing off the whiskey in his glass. "Man gets called out, it's either fight or run, and Pete ain't the running kind."

Irby grinned broadly and nodded. Matt

put his attention on the Huckaby cowhand again.

"What was the argument about?"

Lewis, eyes still on the floor, shook his head. "I ain't for sure —"

"You were sitting right there beside him and you don't know?" Kollister pressed.

"Heard Jake say something about rustling," a man at a table behind the outlaws volunteered. "I expect that's what got them to shooting."

Kollister shifted to Irby. "That it! Harmon accuse you of rustling?"

"Maybe — I ain't for sure just what he was yammering about."

"Or was he in here trying to square up for Travis?"

Pete Irby shook his head. "Wasn't me that plugged him! Ain't saying he didn't have it coming, but it sure wasn't me that done it."

Matt was certain that it had been none of the outlaws, but he was still searching desperately for some clue — a dropped word, a side glance, a gesture — that would put him on the right track to the killer.

"Expect that's what you and Jake came in here for, to shoot the man you thought was the one that killed Travis," Kollister said, coming back to Otto Lewis. "You were aiming to do Mr. Huckaby a good turn." The lawman used the expression the two cow-hands had voiced earlier that day when they'd stopped him.

Otto only grunted. He still sat forward on his chair, but his eyes were now fastened on his dead partner.

"You want to tell me why you and Jake figured it was Pete?"

Lewis straightened up. There was a set look to his face now as he glanced at Irby. "Sure I'll tell you," he said, as if the sight of his lifeless friend had suddenly filled him with the courage to defy Pete Irby and the others. "Me and Jake heard Travis say something about Pete rustling steers. Figured Pete plugged Travis to keep him from telling his pa."

Kollister turned to Irby. "Looks like you're the rustler I was told about."

"Nope, reckon not," Pete replied. "Me and the Huckaby pup had a deal going. We were splitting what I got for the steers he bunched off now and then — down the middle. Was Huckaby steers and he was a Huckaby, so you can't claim it was rustling — and you ain't got no reason to jug me for it."

Kollister gave that thought. "Don't aim to," he said finally.

"And you sure can't do nothing to him

for shooting that bird there on the floor," Vickers pointed out. "Was him or the other fellow. Man's got a right to protect himself."

The truth of it all irked the lawman. Vickers was right, as was Pete Irby — but those were minor items compared to the end result that the shooting could bring about.

"I'm telling you again, Sam, I want you and your bunch gone by morning. Travis's pa said he'd hold off till noon before he brought his men into town after the boy's killer. He's dead certain it's one of your crowd; when he gets wind of this shooting, he's going to be damn sure of it, and he'll forget about waiting till noon. You're not going to be here — savvy?"

Vickers gestured indifferently. "Oh, sure, but I reckon me and my boys could take care of ourselves against them saddle-warmers."

"Well, you're not going to try it here in my town!" Kollister snapped, and turned to Lewis. "And I want you out of here before you can get into more trouble. Load up your friend there and head for home. Couple of you men give him a hand — not any of you," he added to the outlaws.

Otto Lewis had come to his feet and was moving to where Harmon lay. One of the saloon's patrons stepped up, and together the two men lifted the body and carried it outside to where the Diamond H horses were waiting.

Shortly there was the sound of hooves moving off down the street, and the obliging customer reappeared and returned to the bar.

"He's gone," the man said, motioning for a drink. "Sure was heavy."

Kollister nodded his thanks and put his glance on Vickers. "Don't be here in the morning when I make my rounds" he said, and headed for the doorway.

Pistol still in hand, clearly visible on the off-chance that one of the outlaws might undertake a foolish move, he stepped out into the cooling night. The crowd was larger, but it had moved away from the front of the Trail's End to the saloon's hitchrack, which stood off to one side. Likely that was where Harmon and Lewis had tied their horses.

"Marshal — just a moment!" a voice called from down the street.

Matt swore quietly. It was John Craig in company with Hank Beatty.

While he had been waiting inside the saloon, keeping an eye on Irby and the other outlaws while the body of Jake Harmon was being loaded onto his mount, he had been trying to decide what he'd best do. The reaction at the Diamond H when Lewis returned with Harmon would be bitter, and as he'd pointed out to Vickers and the others in the Trail's End, the rancher would likely hold back no longer. He would forget about the noon deadline he had set — or the extension, if Beth had succeeded in persuading him to delay — and, determined on vengeance, would bring his men into town immediately. It could be later that night, or during the early morning hours when the light would be better. He must be prepared for either.

"You arresting Irby for killing that man?" Craig asked as he drew near.

"Nope," Matt replied. "Harmon brought it on himself. Tried to draw on Irby but was too slow. Got that from Deal."

"Might be best to lock him up anyway, let that bunch know the law won't —"

"They've been told to be out of here by morning. Made that double plain this time. I don't want Huckaby to catch them around."

"Can bet he'll be coming now," Beatty said. "First Travis and that Buck Snapp, and now Jake Harmon. What do you aim to do, Marshal?"

"Get ready for them."

Craig brushed nervously at his jaw. "That mean you want them that said they'd help to get their guns and climb up on the roof and —"

"No, no need for that yet. Good chance Huckaby will wait for daylight, but pass the word along to keep their weapons handy and be ready if I give the signal — two quick shots."

"Where'll you be?" Craig asked, signifying his understanding.

"On the street," Kollister said, and moved on.

Reaching the Alamo, Matt turned up onto the porch and entered. Seera, her features strained, met him in the lobby. The worry faded instantly, and was replaced with a welcoming smile.

"Is everything all right?"

"Hard to say," he replied. "Hate having to jump up and run like I did, but at a time like that it's smart to get there quick. Keeps somebody else from getting killed, sometimes."

"I heard there was a killing. Who was it?"

"Cowhand named Harmon. Works for Huckaby," Matt said. "Pete Irby shot him . . . I've got to get my rifle."

Seera trailed him down the hall to his room, waited while he unlocked the door, and then entered with him and stood by silent while he struck a match to the lamp on the dresser. As the light spread, he separated the weapon from several pieces of clothing with which it had been rolled in the blanket and supplied himself with a handful of cartridges from a sack in his saddlebags. The strained look had once more claimed her soft features when he turned to face her.

"What —" she began hesitantly, a thread of fear running through her voice.

He smiled. "Just going to find myself a place along the street to sit and watch. Don't think anything will happen, but I figure it's best to be on the safe side."

"Huckaby, you mean. He may bring his men in after Pete Irby —"

"I'm expecting him anyway," Kollister said, shrugging it off. "He agreed to wait till noon, but this could change that. Just want to be ready."

Seera nodded. "You could use the roof of my porch. We could put a chair out there and —"

He stilled her with a hand on her arm. "Be fine, but I couldn't do that. If they do come in and shooting starts, I'd be putting you in the line of fire — and getting you hurt is the last thing I'd ever want to do."

She lowered her head, and for several moments made no comment. Then she said, "Where will you be? I'll bring coffee and a little something to eat."

"Coffee'll be plenty. There's an empty shack on the other side of the Bonanza —"

"Yes, a bootmaker used to be in it. One day he just loaded up his wagon and drove off."

"I figure to borrow a chair from the saloon and sit out in front of the shack. Can get a good look at the street and everybody coming or going."

Seera frowned. "Will you be alone?"

"Only takes one man to watch, and Craig's got it arranged for help to come if need be. All I have to do is fire a signal — two quick gunshots. If you hear that, stay inside."

The woman nodded, and followed him back into the hall and on into the lobby. He turned to her, seemed about to take her in his arms, but thought better of it.

"Remember now, stay inside if you hear shots," he warned as he started for the door.

Seera smiled. "Take care — I'll have breakfast waiting in the morning early," she said as he stepped out onto the porch.

"Evening, Marshal —"

Kollister paused as a dark shape rose from one of the slatted rocking chairs. It was

Henry Bell.

"Evening," the lawman replied.

"Heard about the shooting. You arresting the man who did the killing?"

"No, he was defending himself. Wasn't exactly a fair match, but he has the law on his side."

Bell shook his head, sighed. "I'm finding it a bit hard to understand the law out here. One man kills another and goes free. Strange. Fellow that was killed — a cowhand. I think somebody said — he worked for this rancher, Huckaby?"

"Right. Seems he took it in his own hands to square up the shooting of Travis Huckaby — the old man's son — this morning. Bit off more'n he could chew," Kollister said, and moved toward the edge of the porch.

"Sad business," Bell murmured. "Do you think the boy's father will be coming in now to square up, as you term it, the killings?"

"No doubt about it. Talked to him late this afternoon. Gave me until noon tomorrow to find the killer, else he was bringing his men in and taking the town apart until he found the killer."

"Have you had any luck finding the killer?"

Matt shrugged. "Hardly had time to think about it, much less do any digging around,"

148

he said, stepping down into the street. "I'm hoping things will ease off in the morning and I can get busy at it."

"Looks to me like you're expecting trouble from Huckaby tonight," Bell said, frowning as he pointed at the rifle hung in the crook of the lawman's arm.

"Learned a long time ago never to take anything for granted," Kollister said. Turning right, he headed off through the half-dark for the shack near the end of the street.

Reaching the Bonanza, he detoured inside and found Bert McAdams, along with three customers and his usual complement of employees. Matt allowed the man to treat him to a drink, explaining what he had in mind for the night. Shortly thereafter, with the chair in his possession, he dropped back to the street and continued on to the old cobbler's quarters to set up his position in front of it.

Shoham was quiet, Kollister realized, probably more so than usual thanks to the pending threat of violence posed by Hiram Huckaby. A few persons appeared along the sidewalks, all en route to one place or another; the strollers who would ordinarily be taking their ease in the pleasant evening hours — as was the custom everywhere — were noticeably absent. There was simply no loitering, not even in front of the saloons.

Around ten o'clock or so three riders appeared at the north end of town. They drew Kollister's close attention at first, but as they traveled the length of the street, it became evident they were headed for Dolly's Place. Each eyed him curiously — sitting in the chair cocked back against the wall of the shack, rifle across his knee — and nodded respectfully as they passed.

They could be Diamond H men, Matt realized after they had gone, so a time later to settle the question in his mind, he walked over to Dolly's and had a look at their horses. None wore a Huckaby brand; while that was not positive proof they were from some other ranch, it seemed likely.

About midnight Seera Ford arrived, bringing a wedge of hot buttered apple pie and a cup of steaming coffee. Persuading her to take his chair, he squatted nearby while he enjoyed the snack and they carried on a desultory conversation. There were things in his mind that Matt wanted to say to the woman, but he found he had now become cautious where she was concerned, perhaps arrising from the recently remembered fact that for him there was only a shadowy future, at best.

When the coffee and pie were gone and

they had run out of topics to discuss, Kollister walked Seera back to the hotel where they lingered briefly in the soft lamplight coming from the lobby. When he returned to his post, Matt wished he could have taken Seera in his arms, held her close and convinced her of how much she had come to mean to him. But it would have been unfair, and he would deny himself his place in heaven — if he were destined for such — before he would hurt her.

The long, quiet hours began. Faint piano music was drifting over from Dolly's, as well as from the Trail's End down the way. The street was now completely deserted beneath a canopy of silver-flecked black velvet, with only lonely squares of window light marking the locations of the saloons yet open for business. The whole town had become a collection of irregularly shaped hulks, alternately silvered and shadowed in the warm night.

Occasionally a dog, disturbed by one thing or another, barked nervously; once the lawman heard the distant, disconsolate howl of a wolf, which served to magnify the forlornness of those hours when old thoughts come out of the past to haunt and unsettle a man's mind and turn him inward.

■ ■ ■ ■

Near dawn, with the town lying in a deep hush except for the ambitious whistling of a meadowlark over behind Craig's, the three cowhands emerged from Dolly's. Again they passed by, this time pointing north. Two gave Matt the customary two-fingers-to-the-hat-brim greeting, but the third — asleep in his saddle — was totally unaware of the moment.

A short time after that, with the first rose and salmon streaks brightening the sky above the eastern horizon, Kollister gathered up the borrowed chair and returned it to the Bonanza, setting it in the space between the batwings and the locked front door.

Other than Seera he'd had no visitors during the night, and had seen no one at close range except her and the trio of cowhands. But that mattered nothing to him; a solitary man by choice, he'd had time to think, doze occasionally for short periods, and now felt ready to face whatever the day might hold for him.

Pleased and relieved that so far there'd been no sign of Huckaby, Kollister angled across the street for his office. He wouldn't need the rifle now, and would leave it in the gun rack. Then he'd drop by the hotel, get a cup of coffee from Seera, and make his rounds. By that time Sam Vickers and his crowd should be gone. If not —

A buckboard had turned into the upper end of the street. Kollister crossed quickly to the door and stepped out onto the landing. It was Beth Huckaby. Seeing him standing in front of the jail, she whipped up her horses as if in a great hurry to talk with him.

Matt frowned. What was bringing her into town so early?

# 12

Seera, carrying the tray upon which was Henry Bell's breakfast, glanced out of the window of the restaurant when she heard the steady beat of passing horses.

Ordinarily it would have been Clara serving the hotel's only other guest, but Seera was keeping the older woman at the kitchen stove this morning to prepare a good meal of steak, eggs and potatoes for Matt. She was certain he would soon present himself — unshaven, irritable and in the advanced stages of hunger — at her door. The thought was filling her with tingling anticipation.

"That the Huckaby girl?" Bell asked, following her line of sight.

Seera set the tray on the table before the elderly man. "Yes," she murmured and crossed to the window.

A frown drew her thick brows together. What was Beth doing in town — and so early? With the possibility of trouble hanging in the air, you'd think she'd stay clear of town. And where was she going?

At that moment Seera saw Kollister in front of the jail. Arms folded across his chest, he appeared to be waiting for the girl. Resentment lifted with Seera. Matt had mentioned in passing that he had encountered and talked with Beth during his return from Diamond H. He had made little of it, seemingly considering it of little importance, and she had dismissed it from her mind. Now she began to have doubts.

In a buckboard, Beth was driving straight down the center of the street and heading for the marshal's office. From the look of it, she had a prearranged meeting with Matt. Seera's resentment increased gradually to a feeling of hurt as she watched the girl. Dressed in riding skirt, white blouse open at the throat, and a bright yellow scarf about her head, she finally wheeled into the rack before the jail.

Immediately Matt stepped up to the vehicle. One hand on the seat's side rail, the other resting on a wheel, he said something to the girl. She nodded in reply and for several minutes the two were engaged in earnest conversation, during which Beth pointed off toward the brushy hills to the south.

"Seen her once before," Bell said. "Wasn't sure she was his daughter."

Seera barely heard, her attention fixed upon Matt who was now climbing up into the buckboard and settling down beside Beth. At once the girl swung the team back into the street and headed in the direction in which she had gestured.

Still frowning, Seera turned from the window and doubled back to the kitchen. What was going on? How could anything with Beth Huckaby — who certainly should not be taken as a friend considering the situation existing between the town and the Huckabys — be so important that Matt would go riding off into the hills with her? He would know full well that his breakfast would be ready and waiting for him at the restaurant.

"He coming?" Clara asked, reaching for a clutch of eggs.

"No — wait," Seera answered. "He's been held up — I don't know for how long."

"Steak's done," the older woman grumbled. "Won't be fit to eat if I have to keep warming it."

Seera shrugged wearily and returned to the dining room. Bell was in need of more coffee. Taking up a small pot, she moved to his table and wordlessly made the refill.

That done, she retraced her steps to the back of the room.

Could there have been more to the meeting between Matt and Beth Huckaby than he'd let on, Seera wondered again. They seemed to be well acquainted for two persons who had just met. And why had they hurried off into the hills, away from town? Matt had intended to start out first thing making the rounds, looking for the outlaws and seeing to it that they had left town or were in the process of doing so. He'd made a point of it being of utmost importance, yet he had chosen for some reason to forget that and go off with Beth.

A burst of angry impatience rolled through Seera. Just what could their going off into the hills have to do with the law? And since when did Beth Huckaby become so comfounded law-abiding — if that was the reason? She'd always been one of those who did what she pleased when she wished, the spoiled daughter of a rich and powerful man who believed she could have anything and anybody she wanted!

Anybody — the word brought a glistening to Seera Ford's eyes and a stab of jealousy to her heart. She'd thought that Matt and she, one day — perhaps —

But she could forget that, she thought,

shrugging again — this time in a gesture of hopeless resignation. She'd lost the first man she had ever loved to a bullet, and now, with that hurt barely healed, she was losing the second to another woman.

It was best to wipe Matt Kollister out of her mind right then — that very instant — and cleanse herself of every thought of him. Life was too short to be put through hell again.

Kollister waited until Beth Huckaby had swung her team to a halt at the hitchrack, then stepped in close to the buckboard. He was puzzled as well as apprehensive at her arrival, which was evidently of some importance.

"Morning," he greeted, as she turned to face him.

"I'm glad I caught you," she replied, the words all coming out in a tumbling hurry. "You said yesterday —"

"This have something to do with your pa?"

"The deadline, you mean, your wanting him to hold off longer? No, not exactly," Beth said. "He wouldn't listen to it. Says the time's set — and it stays"

Kollister rubbed at his whiskery jaw. "A mite hard to figure him. After that killing last night I looked for him to come —"

"Killing?" Beth echoed. "I don't know anything about one, and I'm sure Pa doesn't either. What happened?"

"Cowhand of yours named Jake Harmon got into an argument with Pete Irby, one of the Vickers crowd. Tried to shoot it out with Pete, but came up short."

"Harmon — I think I've heard the name mentioned," Beth said, brushing the incident aside. "It's those outlaws I came to see you about."

Kollister smiled wryly, a bit taken aback by the callousness of the girl's attitude. "What about them? I was just getting ready to go —"

"That's why I hurried in: I wanted to catch you before you started riding herd on them. You said yesterday that if you had some proof you could jail the whole bunch."

He'd said it, Matt recalled, and he'd meant every word. He'd like far better to put Sam Vickers and all of his gang behind bars than proceed with what he was now being forced to do. Driving them out of Shoham accomplished nothing insofar as upholding the law was concerned; they would simply resume their activities elsewhere. But to jail them he needed solid proof.

"Nothing I'd like more."

159

"Well, I've got it," Beth said. "Climb up and I'll take you to where it is."

Kollister threw a glance up the street. Smoke from stoves fired up for the morning meal was twisting thinly up into the clear sky, and there were a few persons abroad. Otherwise, all looked to be quiet at that early hour. Taking a firmer grip on the seat rail, Matt swung up beside the girl.

"I was just telling you about the rustling going on," Beth said as she curved the buckboard back into the street and headed the team south, "and I figured you'd be the most interested in that."

"Breaking the law's a crime no matter what it is," Kollister said, settling back.

"I went to see Zeke Galey last night — he's one of the old hands on the ranch. He's sort of retired. Pa just lets him stay on, do what he pleases. I remembered hearing him say something about rustlers a while back, but I didn't pay any mind to him. I guess I thought it was just talk. He didn't tell Pa about it, and I suppose that's why I never put any stock in it. But last night I got him to come out with everything he knew — the truth."

"Part of that being that your brother was in with Pete Irby selling cattle on the side."

160

Beth stared at Kollister. "How'd you know that?"

"It's what got Jake Harmon killed. Maybe he didn't have it exactly straight, but he did know Irby had a deal of some kind with Travis."

"I see. If you already knew that, why didn't you go ahead and jail him?"

"Takes more proof than the words of a dead man to make a charge like that stick. And your brother being in on it, there'd be some on a jury who'd say it wasn't exactly rustling — the stock being Huckaby cattle." Matt paused, glanced over his shoulder. The settlement was no longer visible, hidden now by a roll of hills. "How far do we have to go to get to this place you're talking about?"

"It'll be about two miles, according to Zeke. There'll be a shack near a spring — they do the butchering there."

Kollister fell silent while he considered Beth Huckaby's words. If she knew what she was talking about — and her knowledge was second-hand — it could be what he needed to put the Vickers gang behind bars — if they were still in town by the time he returned. They could have pulled out, having obeyed his order, which is what he expected; but he found himself hoping that

161

they, at least Vickers and Pete Irby and the other mainstays, had ignored his warning and were still around.

"There's the shack —"

Kollister brought his attention back to Beth. She was pointing to a small structure set well back in the brush and small trees of a hollow. Nearby, the bright green of willows and the other lush growth marked the location of the spring.

"Nobody around," Matt said. "That'll give us a chance to look things over good."

"You'll find the hides buried somewhere behind the place," Beth said as they both came down from the buckboard.

"Hides will prove where the beef came from," Kollister said, "but I'll need more than that. I'll have to catch them doing the butchering — and it'll help to know who they're selling the meat to."

"Seth Wheeler, for one," the girl said bluntly.

Matt halted, turned to her, momentary disbelief filling his eyes. He should not be surprised, he knew; more than once he'd found the person least suspected of a crime to be the guilty party.

"Good. Getting him to tell a judge that he bought meat from Irby and the others mixed up in it with him will go a long way towards putting a rope around their necks. Let's get those hides located so we'll know for certain what we're talking about, then we'll go back to town and I'll deputize some men to come out here, set up a watch —"

A distant crackle of gunshots came to them through the warm, motionless air. Matt halted, glanced toward Shoham. He could not see the settlement because of the intervening hills, but the shooting was taking place there, he was certain. The realization of what it undoubtedly meant brought him pivoting about to face the girl

"This some of your doing?" he demanded harshly. "You sucker me off down here so's your pa and his hired guns could ride into town and draw blood for Travis and those other two?"

Beth stiffened and a sharpness edged her voice. "I don't know anything about it! And I never suckered you anywhere — I brought you here because I wanted to help."

Kollister stared at her for several moments and then abruptly shook his head. "Maybe — but there's no time to talk about it now," he said tersely, and started for the buckboard at a run. "Come on! I've got to get back there fast!"

## 13

The Trail's End again, Matt observed, lean-ing forward, legs braced to prevent being thrown out of the wildly swaying buckboard. Reins in one hand, whip in the other, he drove the team full tilt down the street. A considerable crowd had gathered in front of the saloon, and along the sidewalks groups of people had collected and were convers-ing excitedly. Voices shouted at both of them as they raced by, some filled with anger, oth-ers expressing relief at Matt's arrival.

Reaching the area in front of the saloon, Matt brought the heaving team to a stop. Thrusting the lines into Beth's hands, he dropped to the ground.

"Better get out of here," he warned, tak-ing quick note of the hating glances cast at the girl, and turned away.

His jaw tightened. Five men lay dead on the porch of the Trail's End and in the nar-row strip of ground separating the saloon from the Palace Hotel. Beyond, making use of the landing of the small building housing the town physician and the barber, a squat individual in shirt sleeves and baggy pants — evidently the doctor — was attending a wounded man.

"Where the hell you been?"

Kollister turned. John Craig, features dark, his mouth a taut line, had separated from the men standing near the motionless bodies and was hurrying toward him.

"Down the road a piece," Matt replied. "I —"

"Well, by God, you ought to've been here tending to your job instead of out there in the woods with that Huckaby woman!" Craig shouted. "We've had a regular massacre!"

Kollister, brushing the man off, pressed on by him and halted beside the dead men. It had indeed been a shootout between the Vickers bunch and the Diamond H crew. The dead were Pete Irby, Billy Blue, and one of the outlaws that he did not know. It had cost the Diamond H Otto Lewis and another cowhand. The wounded man being looked after appeared to be another Huckaby rider.

"Could've been worse, Marshall," Simon Deal said, stepping up to Kollister's side.

165

"Was four more of them from Huckaby's — seven in all — and they —"

"Huckaby leading them?" Matt cut in.

"No, didn't see him. They come walking in here big as you please and spoiling for trouble. Wasn't hardly nobody in the place, so they turned around and started back out — was going to the Palace, I expect. Run smack dab into Vickers and his boys right outside the door, and all hell busted loose."

"Vickers get hit?"

"Nope, don't think so. Him and Calico and a couple others come running through here when it was all over and ducked out the back. I figure it was Pete them cowhands was after, getting back at him for killing Jake Harmon."

"Still say you should've been on the job looking out for the town," Craig's voice cut in. He had followed the lawman and was now standing directly behind him. "We all knew this was coming."

"There anybody else hit — any of the townspeople, I mean?" Kollister asked.

"Fellow standing there in front of Ferlin Webb's got nicked by a stray bullet, and there was a couple of windows busted in Levi Marcus's place across the street," Deal replied, "I reckon we were real lucky. Was like a hailstorm of lead around here for a couple of minutes."

"And I'm still saying if you'd been doing the job we hired you to do instead of trotting off into the hills with the Huckaby girl, this maybe wouldn't've happened," Craig muttered doggedly.

Kollister paused, glanced about. The crowd had increased and was milling around, seemingly fascinated by the dead bodies lying on the saloon's porch and in the dust. Webb had now put in his appearance, as had several other members of the town council — Yates, McAdams and Hank Beatty. Matt looked for Seera Ford and failed to locate her, but there was so much confusion that she could have been hidden in the shifting crowd.

"Why'd you go off with her?" Craig continued. "Told me you aimed to see that Vickers and his bunch had pulled out first thing this morning. Instead —"

"Let it drop, Craig," Kollister said, finally fed up with the man's continual complaining.

"Little hard for me to do that," the merchant said. "I feel responsible to the people for hiring you. I told them you'd see that Shoham was a safe place to live. It's looking more'n more to me like we'd be better off to find —"

"If you want my star you can have it right now!" Matt snapped.

"He don't!" Oren Yates said hurriedly. "None of us want that — John's just sort of upset."

"John's expecting too much from one man," Webb added. "Guess maybe we all are because we never had a good lawman in this town, and we figure he ought to be the whole Texas Ranger outfit and the U.S. army rolled into one! I expect he had good reason to be with Beth Huckaby, and in good time he'll tell us about it."

"I reckon he will," Yates said, "but that's done with, same as this shooting. Point is, what do we do now?"

"Expect we'd best leave that up to the marshal," McAdams said, "him having experience and the like and —"

The Bonanza owner broke off as a tall man in a dark suit, followed by two others carrying several stretchers, pushed through the crowd.

"Here's Conroy," a voice said.

The gathering around the fallen outlaws and cowhands quickly pulled back, allowing the late arrivals — Shoham's undertaker and his assistants — to step in and start the removal of the bodies.

Kollister watched in moody silence. Had

he been there, he could have prevented the shootout; it would simply have been a matter of heading off the riders from the Diamond H and turning them back. They had come of their own accord, he now believed, and without the knowledge of Beth Huckaby. Hiram, too, must have been unaware of what his riders had undertaken, otherwise he would have been a member of the vengeance party.

But it was done, as Oren Yates had said, and the question now was what the town should do next. The information concerning the rustling that had been given him by Beth was of value, but it would have to be put on the back of the stove for the time being; they just might end up with no outlaws to punish if Hiram Huckaby was permitted to have his way.

"You figure that Diamond H bunch will be back looking for Sam Vickers and the rest of his crowd?" John Craig asked of everyone in general. The merchant had calmed, and anger no longer tinged his words.

"Can bet on it," Kollister said. "This is a regular war now, and you can look for them to be showing up with every gun they've got."

"That'll sure be bad," Simon Deal said.

"This time there's liable to be some decent folks killed — not just nicked."

"That's what we've got to keep from happening," Matt said.

"How?" Craig wanted to know. "How are we going to stand off maybe a dozen gunfighters?"

"I'm going to start by locking up Vickers and his bunch — whoever's left. That'll keep them out of the way. I want them there anyhow; aim to charge them with cattle rustling — thanks to Beth Huckaby — if we can keep them alive."

"Beth Huckaby?" Webb echoed. "That why you rode off with her in that buckboard this morning?"

"She was taking me to where I could get the proof. Nothing I'd like better than to put Sam and his crowd behind bars —"

"We hang rustlers around here, Marshal."

Kollister looked around at the speaker, a man in the gathering whom he did not know. The undertaker had removed the bodies and the crowd had thinned out to where only a half dozen bystanders remained along with the handful of council members.

"Whatever the judge says," Matt replied with a shrug. "There'll be no lynching."

"Won't have to bother with them if we let

that Diamond H outfit have their way," the same man observed. "Why don't we just let old Hiram and his Enforcers take care of them? All we'd have to do is just stand back and let them go at it."

"And get the town all shot to hell and maybe three or four people killed — that what you want, Dan?" McAdams demanded. "You best listen to the marshal. Go ahead," the saloon man added, nodding to Kollister.

"Next move'd be to send word to Huckaby, tell him to back off, that Vickers and his bunch are my prisoners and he's to forget about them."

"Which maybe he will and maybe he won't," Craig said.

"Like as not, he won't," the lawman agreed, "but when there's shooting in sight it's a smart idea to try and head it off any way you can."

"And if he comes on anyway?"

"We'll have men on the roofs, and everywhere else that'll make a good post."

"And you — where'll you be?"

"In the street. I'll meet Huckaby, let him take a look at the guns pointing down at him and his men, and tell him the best thing he can do is ride on out."

"Could work," Craig agreed. "Who you

figuring to send out to tell Huckaby that he ain't to come in?"

"You sure better not go yourself," Ferlin Webb warned. "You might get there, but I sure'n hell wouldn't bet on your getting back!"

"Best I stay here," Kollister said, nodding. "Just could be Huckaby's already on his way, and I want to be around when — and if — he comes."

"Hell, he'll be coming," Craig said heavily. "Ain't no doubt of that. How about sending him?" he continued, jerking a thumb at the Diamond H rider standing in front of the doctor's office. The physician had finished his ministrations and was giving the cowhand some final instructions.

"Be fine," Matt said. "We know he'll get there."

"I'll tell him what you want Huckaby to know," Craig volunteered, and immediately cut away to intercept the man, now moving toward his horse.

"Next thing's some deputies," Kollister stated. "Pass the word along, have anybody that's interested come to my office and I'll —"

A rider suddenly pounded into the upper end of the street, horse running at full gallop as the man applied spurs and leather mercilessly.

"Doc!" he yelled, catching sight of the physician just entering his quarters. "You got to get to the ranch quick! Somebody went and shot Miss Beth while she was driving home. Best you hurry — looks like she's hurt real bad!"

Shock rolled through Matt Kollister. It would have happened right after the girl drove off — just after he'd sent her on in the belief that it wasn't safe in town for her.

"God in heaven!" he heard Yates say in a breathless sort of voice. "The fat's in the fire for sure now! Old Hiram's bound to figure one of them outlaws done it!"

"And like as not it was," Beatty declared. "Shooting her'll hit him where it'll hurt most. What had we better do, Marshal?"

"Get ready," Kollister said grimly. "Doubt if we'll even have an hour before Huckaby and his bunch shows up."

The lawman paused and spun to face Craig, returning after his conversation with the injured rider. Before the store owner could speak, Matt said, "The men you got lined up — get them on the roofs as soon as you can. Tell them they're not to use their guns unless I give the word. And the man you've put on the roof of The Emporium — we want a warning from him the moment he spots Huckaby. All hell's going to bust loose unless we can get it headed off!"

Immediately the men separated and hurried off toward their places of business. Oren Yates pulled up abruptly.

"Them deputies you wanted, I —"

"Forget it," Kollister replied. "If I can find Vickers, I'll try to talk him into letting me lock him and the others up for safekeeping, but I doubt I'll have any luck doing either."

The feedstore man nodded soberly and hurried on. It would be a waste of time hunting up Vickers and appealing to him and his men to surrender and allow themselves to be locked in the jail; they'd certainly not listen to what he'd have to say about sparing the town bloodshed, Matt thought, heading off down the street. Like all men of their following, they would be interested only in squaring accounts, in this case with Huckaby's Diamond H. But, for the sake of the town, Kollister reckoned he'd best try and find Vickers and do what he could.

He would get his rifle first, he decided, continuing steadily along the quiet, deserted street for the jail. He preferred carrying only his pistol, but if a confrontation developed into a war, the advantage of the long gun's magazine — seventeen bullets before reloading — could not be overlooked.

Reaching his office, Matt glanced over his shoulder. Two men were now visible on the roof of Simon Deal's saloon, and someone was placing a ladder against the wall of the Palace Hotel that would permit access to its topmost level. That word of the oncoming crisis had spread quickly was evident; doors of all business houses, as well as the few residences nearby, were closed with blinds drawn, and the sidewalks were empty — all of which gave Shoham a desolate, abandoned look.

Entering his office, Matt retrieved the rifle from the rack where he had placed it. Thrusting a handful of cartridges into a pocket, he then dropped back to the street. There was nothing to do now but wait, and watch. The sentry on the roof of The Emporium — the furthest building to the north and therefore the one nearest to the road upon which Huckaby and his Diamond H gunmen would first appear — had been instructed by Craig to sound a warning when he saw the rancher approaching. Such would allow everyone to get set.

Kollister, moving slowly back up the street, came abreast the Alamo. Seeing Seera Ford standing in the window of the restaurant, he realized that he had skipped the breakfast the woman had been preparing for him. In the hard crush of rapidly succeeding incidents that morning, he had simply forgotten all about eating. Veering from course, he stepped up onto the hotel's porch, entered its lobby, and made his way into the restaurant. Seera turned to face him, her attitude cool and distant.

"Sorry about the breakfast," he said. "Got tied up, and then things started happening —"

"I know — I saw you leave with Beth Huckaby," she said icily.

Propping his rifle against a table, Matt studied her closely. "Was hoping to jug Vickers and his crowd for rustling and head off this showdown that's coming today. Beth was taking me to where I'd find proof."

Seera shrugged and resumed staring out of the window. "You don't owe me any explanation. How is she? Have you heard?"

"No. I doubt the doctor is back yet. From what that cowhand said, she was in bad shape, though."

"Too bad," Seera murmured. "Do you want to eat now?"

"No time for that, but I could use a cup of coffee," he replied, frowning. As she turned away he laid his hand on her arm. "I'd like to know what's wrong?"

"Wrong?" she echoed, pulling free and starting for the back of the room. "There's nothing wrong."

"The hell there ain't!" he snapped impatiently. "I get busy and don't get a chance to show up for breakfast, and I find you a stranger!"

Seera halted at the table near the kitchen, selected a cup and reached for the pot of coffee. "This is cold — I'll get some from the stove —"

"Let it ride!" Kollister said harshly. Seizing her by the arm, he spun her about. "I'm more interested in getting things straight with you!"

Again Seera pulled away. Looking down, she shook her head. "There's nothing to be —"

"If seeing me with Beth Huckaby's got you all riled up, you're being foolish. All there was — or is — between us is business, law business. She doesn't mean a whit to me."

Seera raised her head to face him. Her eyes were glistening. "Matt — can I believe that?"

"Every word."

"I've had enough grief for one lifetime; I can't stand more."

Kollister took the woman in his arms and

held her close. "It will never come from me," he said.

For a long minute she clung to him; then, pulling back, she smiled. "I'm sorry. With all the terrible problems facing you I had no right —"

"If you feel about me the way I do about you, then you had every right," he cut in. "I don't want anything to come between us, and talking out a misunderstanding is the best way to clear it up. I sure hate upsetting you."

"It's all right — I was being foolish. I'll get you some coffee."

As Seera turned to go into the kitchen, Matt retraced his steps to the window and let his eyes run the street. It was still deserted along the sidewalks, but he could see more men on the roofs of the buildings. That was good; Craig had his sentries in place well ahead of time.

A sound in the hotel lobby brought the lawman around. It was Henry Bell. Evidently the investor had come down from his room to find a chair to settle into where he would await the noon meal or the excitement that would take place — whichever occurred first. Kollister smiled wryly: there were those, he'd found, who enjoyed standing on the edge of violence and taking a grisly pleasure in seeing men die. Bell, he reckoned, could be counted among them.

Seera appeared bringing a cup of coffee in each hand. Moving up beside Matt, she surrendered one cup, and then looked at the abandoned street.

"It's so quiet, like before a big storm," she murmured. "Folks are expecting the worst."

"That's how it will be — a war — unless I can stop it before it gets started."

Seera frowned. "Alone? I don't see —"

"I aim to be waiting for Huckaby and his men when they get to the edge of town, to try and talk him into letting the law handle things. Figured I had a good chance until somebody shot Beth. That sort of leaves me without much hope.

"But I figure maybe Vickers and the rest of the outlaw bunch — what's left of them — will back off and keep out of sight. They're short-handed after Irby and Blue and that other one got killed, and that could make Sam do a bit of thinking. Some of his boys may have even pulled out, and that would put him in a worse tight for guns."

"Then, if they stay hid out and you can make Hiram Huckaby see reason —"

"We'll have it licked," Kollister said cheerfully, but there was little conviction in his tone. "I want you to be sure and stay in here out of the way. Later, we've got some talking to do. You know where I stand with the law. Could be I'll ask you to pull stakes and go to Mexico with me."

"Anywhere you want — anytime," she said in a low voice.

Kollister regretted his words the moment he'd uttered them. "Forget what I said. It's not right that I ask that — I can't expect you to give up your life here, all you've got, and go with me. It would be too much of a sacrifice, and I can't offer you anything."

"Only what I want most," Seera said. "Nothing else matters."

He shook his head slowly and once more let his gaze probe the street. Finally he said, "We'll see. Soon as things settle down here we'll hash it out. I figure the job I've got here will end today — or maybe tomorrow morning if luck's with me."

At once Seera's features darkened with concern. "I — I wish we could just pack up and go now, that you wouldn't have to face Huckaby — and maybe the shooting. Matt, I'm afraid —"

"Don't be. I've been through this before and I'm an old hand at looking out for my hide. You just be sure and stay —"

Two quick gunshots broke the hush that hung over the town. Immediately Kollister

180

set his cup on a close-by table.

"Damn — they're here sooner than I figured!" he said. "No time to do anything." Drawing Seera close with his free arm, he kissed her.

"Be careful, for my sake — for both of us," she murmured as he turned.

"Can bet on it," Kollister replied, and hurried toward the restaurant's entrance and the street beyond.

# 14

Barely nodding to Bell, Kollister reached the center of the street in a dozen lengthy strides. The cattlemen had moved in fast. Hiram Huckaby was in the lead of the party; to his left rode Charlie Marshall, on his right was Ed Waggoner; Chet Jones, Dutch Schultz and Aubrey McEvee followed a yard or two behind. All were staring straight ahead, features grimly set.

Walking slowly, Matt moved forward to meet them. When the riders were abreast of the Trail's End, he raised a hand and the Diamond H men came to a halt.

"Step aside, Marshal," Huckaby said coldly. "I'm here to settle with them damn outlaws the town's been cozying up to. They killed my boy and they tried to kill my daughter, besides all the other devilment they've caused. I ain't —"

"Up to me to take care of them —"

"You ain't done much good so far,"

182

Huckaby cut in. "Told me you'd find Travis's killer and lock him up. What I've been told, you ain't done nothing about it yet."

"Haven't had much chance. Your men riding in here and taking things into their own hands hasn't given me any time," Kollister replied. "I seem to recollect that you were giving me until noon before you —"

"That all changed when one of them lousy bastards shot my girl," the rancher shouted, breaking in again. "Now, there ain't no use of you getting yourself mixed up in this, Marshal. Just you go take yourself a little ride."

Matt shook his head. "Can't do that. My job is to keep the peace, and that's just what I figure to do."

Turning his head slightly, he threw a glance at the jail. Huckaby's sudden arrival had caught him unready. He had of course expected the rancher to react, but not quite so quickly. If he'd had time to find Sam Vickers, do his best to persuade him to surrender, or even pull out, the town might be spared a wholesale shoot-out. But he'd failed, and now all he could do was talk — and bluff.

"Hate to hear that, son," Huckaby said in a more kindly tone. "Sort of took a liking to you. You showed plenty of guts coming up to my place, but I ain't letting that stand in my way. I come here to square accounts, and I ain't going home till I do."

Kollister shook his head. "There'll be no shooting here, Huckaby. Want you to understand that."

Charlie Marshall leaned forward on his saddle. The heat was already making itself felt, and was showing in the damp shine on his hard-set face.

"You figure you're big enough to stop all six of us?" he asked in a taunting tone.

Kollister's shoulders stirred. "I'll sure as hell stop you and a couple more," he said coolly, and let his gaze reach up to the rooftops along the street. "The men I've got staked out up there'll take care of the rest."

Marshall laughed. "You betting on them counter-jumpers? Hell, they'll end up shooting themselves! We seen them riding in; they don't count for sour apples."

"You'll find out you're wrong," the lawman said in a firm voice. "There's law in this town now and everybody's backing it. I want you all to turn around and ride out."

The street was deserted, except for the men partly visible on the roofs, and totally quiet. While most doors had closed quickly upon the approach of Huckaby and his men, there were a few that were cracked sufficiently to allow whoever stood beyond to view the proceedings. Tension was mounting steadily; Kollister could feel it. He had no idea where Vickers and the other outlaws might be, or what they had in mind, but he realized that he must get Huckaby and his riders off the street and on their way back to the Diamond H before something could happen. Each passing moment brought the actuality of bloody violence a step closer.

"Like to say I'm sorry about your daughter getting shot, and I'm hoping she's not bad hurt. But running down whoever did it is up to me — not you, same as finding and jailing the man who killed your son. You're to leave it up to me, and you're to do what I tell you. Now take your men and get out."

Huckaby, hands folded and resting in his lap, glanced about while the big horse he was riding stirred restlessly. After a bit the rancher shrugged.

"Done you one favor already, Marshal. In my book you ain't entitled to another, so back off and let me go about what I'm aiming to do."

"Favor? What was it?"

"Travis. I should've rode right in here and cleaned out this town when he got killed. I didn't — I listened to you, told you I'd hold off. Then three of my hired hands get shot."

"Best you remember it was them that started it," Matt said.

"No, come down to bedrock, it was Travis's killing that started it, and now my girl getting bushwhacked is going to mean the end to it. I've plumb had enough."

"You've still got no reason to —"

"Mister, I've got every reason!" Huckaby said in a flat, clear voice. "Truth is, I have had for quite a spell."

"You talking about the trouble between you — your ranch — and the town?"

"Ain't so much the town maybe, it's that bunch of renegades that hangs around it that's caused all the trouble."

Kollister's eyes caught a slight movement at the far corner of the Palace Hotel — a man, he thought, but he could not be sure. Since it was beyond the rancher and his riders, it had gone unnoticed by them.

"You can forget about them," the lawman said. "Was one of the things I was hired to do: drive them out of here or jail them."

"Yeh, you'll be doing that just about as quick as you jugged the man that killed my boy."

Matt's attention drifted slightly to cover Charlie Marshall and the other riders —

the Enforcers, as they had been dubbed. All had slowly brought their horses about until they were in a position to watch the hushed street from every angle. They pretended to disdainfully ignore the riflemen on the roofs of the buildings, but Matt noticed they cast wary glances at them from time to time.

"It'll be done," Kollister said doggedly. "All I need is for you to pull out and let me go about my job."

Huckaby unlocked his hands, and let them drop to his sides. Again there was motion near the Palace — this time in the brush growing between it and the building housing the barber shop and doctor's office.

"It ain't good us a-setting here like ducks on a pond, Mr. Huckaby," Schultz said nervously, belying the bravado he and his brother Enforcers were displaying. "Why don't we just climb down and start rooting out them bastards?"

"Dutch is right," Waggoner added, wiping at the sweat on his seamed face. "I'm getting goosey as hell doing this sitting and waiting."

Matt Kollister's arms, crossed before him, unfolded like Huckaby's; his hands sank to his sides. All hell could break out at any instant, for he knew he could not permit Huckaby and his hired guns to dismount and start a search for Vickers and his followers — who, at that exact moment, could be lining up their gunsights on the rancher and his men.

"Telling you once more, Huckaby, take your hired help and move on. This is my town and I won't have you turning it into a battlefield."

"Your town!" the rancher echoed, and laughed. "The man's been here a couple of days and already figures he owns the place!"

"I do, as far as keeping the peace is concerned."

"Which you ain't doing. Already got a half a dozen killings on your hands. If you was doing the job right, you'd'a jugged them renegades soon as you pinned on that star."

"You don't jail a man on reputation alone. Takes some proof of them breaking the law."

"Hell!" Huckaby said in disgust, "I expect every one of them's wanted for something."

"Probably, but there's no records here in the marshal's office, and it'll take time to send out word and do some asking. A man does things according to the law — or the law's worthless."

Matt paused. He had forgotten himself. He was speaking as if he were a regular, bona fide lawman performing his sworn duty, instead of a fugitive on the run for

Mexico — a run which could resume at any moment should Fred Larkin come into the scene.

"You sure do go out of your way to treat them nice and kind," Huckaby said dryly.

"I'm doing it the right way: a man has to be proven guilty before you can hang him. I think I've got the proof to do that, or at least I've got a start at it. Was my plan to lock the whole bunch up in jail, hold them for the judge —"

"You can forget that! Get out of my way and I'll see they get all the trial they need!" the rancher shouted, and raked spurs across the flanks of his horse.

Kollister's pistol came up smooth and fast, little more than a glinting blur in the morning sunlight. Huckaby jerked his mount to a stop; Marshall and the other men with him tensed, awed by the speed and ease with which the lawman had drawn his weapon, but bolstered by sheer number — maintaining their arrogant front of confidence nevertheless.

"Move on, Huckaby," Matt ordered quietly. "You're not turning this town into a shooting gallery."

The rancher eased back in his saddle. Pulling off his hat, he mopped at the sweat on his forehead. "Son, throwing down on me like you just done — in my book that's the same as siding in with them renegades."

"Not siding with anybody," Kollister stated in a cold voice. "I'm trying to stop some killing before it gets started."

"Yeh, maybe that's what you're telling yourself, but you're plumb foolish," the rancher countered. "You got no call to mix in this — it's purely Diamond H business."

A flash of sunlight on metal in a window of the Palace trapped Matt's eye, as did motion in the passageway lying between the old hotel and the adjacent Trail's End. Charlie Marshall and Aubrey McEvee noticed, too. Abruptly the movement resolved into a man with a rifle — Calico Hays. The shine in the hotel window became another man, also holding a weapon.

"Look out!" Kollister yelled at Huckaby as realization flooded through him. "Ambush!" he added, but the word was drowned out in a blast of gunfire.

# 15

In the next fragment of time, Matt saw Hiram Huckaby throw up his arms, rock sideways on his saddle, and start to fall. Nearby, Charlie Marshall was buckling and going down, as was Chet Jones. Waggoner, Schultz and McEvee were hurling themselves to the ground and endeavoring to keep behind their milling horses.

A bullet ripped through Kollister's shirt sleeve. Yelling to the townsmen positioned on the roofs of the buildings to hold their fire, he dropped flat into the dust and tried to locate the marksmen. The man at the window of the Palace and the one he'd spotted in the passageway alongside the Trail's End were no longer to be seen, but puffs of smoke were spurting from the doorway of the old hotel and from the brush beyond the building which housed the doctor's office and the barber shop. It was evident that Vickers and his outlaw friends were holed up all along that side of the street. Huckaby and his Enforcers had ridden into a trap.

Another bullet dug into the loose dirt near Matt's shoulder; he threw an answering shot at the tell-tale bulge of smoke — this one from the trash-littered space between the Trail's End and Ferlin's Gun & Saddle Shop. Dutch Schultz and Waggoner also began to open up, while Huckaby, face down, rolled over onto his left side and dragged out his pistol to join in the return fire.

There were no signs of life in either Charlie Marshall or Jones, who lay where they had fallen in the street, now filling with drifting smoke and dust. McEvee, who sprawled close by the two, seemed content to remain motionless. He was unhurt as near as Matt could tell.

More guns broke loose along the street. Some, it seemed to Kollister, belonged to the townsmen on the roofs. Bullets were digging into the dry, baked soil, sending up small geysers of yellow powder. One of the horses nickered suddenly, then staggered and fell — almost upon Hiram Huckaby. The two remaining animals bolted immediately, and galloped off in pursuit of those that had trotted off at the outbreak of shooting.

"We ain't got a chance here!" Dutch Schultz yelled frantically crawling in beside the rancher, now sheltered by the dead horse.

Huckaby, on his back as he reloaded his weapon, only shook his head. The front of his shirt was stained with blood and dust, and there was a slackness to his features, but his eyes were bright and accusing as he glanced briefly at Kollister.

He was being blamed for the ambush, Matt realized, and he reckoned he could be held accountable to some degree. But that was beside the point at that moment. It was certain death there — pinned down as they were — in the middle of the street.

"Schultz is right!" he shouted, gathering his legs under him. "Stay low, and make a run for —"

Abruptly, Ed Waggoner lunged to his feet. Snapping a shot in the general direction of the outlaws, he dashed for the downed horse. He covered half a dozen strides when he halted stiffly as bullets slammed into him and knocked him to the ground. Taking advantage of the moment, Matt gained his footing and raced across the short distance to the passageway lying between the general store and Oren Yates's place.

Comparatively safe from bullets, both

those of the outlaws and his own men, Matt took stock of the situation. Huckaby and Schultz would be all right for the time being; McEvee, too, as long as he continued to play dead. But the rancher was wounded and should have help quickly. As far as the outlaws were concerned, they were having it all their way. Scattered along the west side of the street, firing from well-concealed positions, they probably had sustained no casualties or injuries. And, they would continue to enjoy that advantage until Huckaby and his two remaining men were out of the street.

It was up to him to bring it to an end. Kollister faced that fact: As a lawman, he could not permit it to continue. Three dead already — Huckaby, perhaps, mortally wounded; the odds were also good that before it was over, McEvee and Dutch Schultz would also die.

Matt let his eyes probe the buildings on the opposite side of the street where the outlaws had taken cover. He guessed his one chance to do anything would be to cross over and get behind the structures. Once that was accomplished, he could then make his way along the alleylike area that ran in back of them and move in on the outlaws from the rear. He'd find some in passageways, some in the weeds and brush; there would be others in the old Palace Hotel, and possibly in the Trail's End. It would be a one-at-a-time job, and that would not only require considerable time but could also prove extremely difficult. The key would be Sam Vickers; if he could locate, disarm and march him out in view of his friends, there was a chance they would quit.

It was only a chance, Kollister had to admit, but it was his best bet. It meant that he would need to move carefully down the alley, keeping out of sight while checking each of the passageways and all other hiding places along the buildings. The continuous shooting by the outlaws would help, as the reports of their weapons and the small puffs of smoke would —

"Damn you, Huckaby!"

The shout came from the direction of the Alamo Hotel, near directly opposite. Kollister came about and saw Henry Bell, pistol in hand, running toward the rancher who was all but completely hidden by the body of the horse. Huckaby, again on his back with his head resting on the animal's belly, was at that moment thumbing cartridges into his empty weapon. He raised himself slightly at the sound of Bell's frenzied cry.

"I'm settling with you once and for all, you damn cheat!" the man continued, and fired.

The bullet missed the rancher, but drove into the luckless Schultz, who jolted and then lay motionless. Huckaby, helpless, continued to press shells into his pistol but was having a hard time of it. The outlaws, surprised also by the unexpected interruption, held their fire.

"I got your boy and I got your girl, and now I'm killing you!" Bell screamed, triggering his weapon again. "You cheated me out of my life, now I'm getting what's due!"

"Bell!" Kollister shouted, stepping forward and leveling his pistol at the man — a hatless, coatless, disheveled figure running erratically toward the center of the street. "Drop your gun!"

"No!" the man yelled back over a shoulder. "I've been twenty years finding him, and I'm not letting him get away now. He cheated me out of everything I had!"

Raising his weapon, Bell got off another shot at the helpless rancher. Again the bullet, fired in haste by a none-too-skilled hand, was wide. Once more he cocked his weapon, slowed his steps and leveled it.

"Bell — no!" Kollister warned.

The man whirled, fired directly at the lawman, but missed. Ignoring the failure, Bell pivoted and aimed point-blank at Huckaby. The rancher, weapon now ready, was endeavoring to twist about to where he could face the enraged Bell. He would not be in time, and at such close range Bell would not miss. Pressing the trigger of his own forty-five, Matt halted Henry Bell in his tracks. The impact of the bullet knocked the man to his knees; he hung there briefly, shouting unintelligible words at Hiram Huckaby, and then sprawled full length into the dust.

Immediately a flurry of shooting broke out, and a bullet dug into the ground at Kollister's feet, while another thudded dully into the wall of the feedstore behind him. He felt the sting of yet another as it sliced across his forearm before he could jerk back. Suddenly, he was conscious that — in his efforts to halt Henry Bell from taking vengeance on Huckaby for some wrong done in the past — he had exposed himself to the outlaws.

Huckaby, pistol ready, had resumed his firing. Doggedly matching the outlaws as best he could with his one weapon, he was aided by a scattering of shots from the rooftops. Two more dead, the lawman thought — Schultz and Henry Bell. And it was Bell, not any of the outlaws as Huckaby presumed, who was the man guilty of killing Travis and making an attempt on Beth's life. The rancher would be realizing that now, and if word, somehow, could be —

A sudden hammer of hoofs echoed through the ragged shooting. A half dozen riders swept in from the road leading to Huckaby's. They veered sharply as the outlaws met their arrival with a hail of bullets, and rushed on to gain safety behind The Emporium. Kollister swore deeply; more Diamond H men. Now the war would start all over again, and his chances for stopping it would end — unless he could stop Huckaby's riders, turn them back. Wheeling, Matt ran the length of Craig's General Store to the alley behind it, and there turned toward The Emporium.

Huckaby's men were just leaving their saddles, yanking rifles from boots, under the leadership of a tall, angular man, apparently the ranch foreman.

"Hold up — all of you!" Kollister shouted.

The riders halted uncertainly, turning to the tall man who faced Matt. "Telling you now, friend," he said, "if Mr. Huckaby's dead, you're going to pay —"

"He came here looking for trouble, and he got it," Kollister snapped, brushing at the sweat on his forehead. "He's hurt, but he's alive. Now, I want you —"

"How about the others? They all dead?"

"One called McEvee's still alive far as I know. Rest are dead."

"Can thank you for that," the tall man said in a bitter tone. "Evans, there," he added, jerking a thumb at one of the cowhands, "was riding in, saw what was happening, and come to fetch me. Said you stopped the boss and the others right out there in the middle of the street so that outlaw gang could open up on them."

"Not exactly how it was. I stopped them, tried to make Huckaby turn around and go back to his ranch and leave Sam Vickers and his crowd up to me. Wouldn't listen. When those outlaws opened up, they were shooting at me, too."

"They doing all that shooting now at Mr. Huckaby and McEvee?"

Kollister nodded. "Probably Huckaby. McEvee's been playing dead, still is unless —"

"Then we're going out there and side him, bring him back if he's bad hurt —"

"You do, and you'll wind up dead like Marshall and the others," Matt cut in. "The outlaws are holed up along the other side of the street, and you'll be in the open. I want you all to stay out of it."

"And just let them keep shooting till the boss is dead? Not much —"

"I'm going to cross over, get in behind Vickers and his crowd, and try and make them back off. Huckaby will be willing to call it off; he knows now that it wasn't one of them that killed Travis and shot Beth."

"What?"

"That's right. It was a man by the name of Bell. Had some kind of a grudge against Huckaby from twenty years back. Admitted shooting Travis and Beth, and was going after Huckaby himself when I stopped him."

"Kill him?" the tall rider asked, frowning.

"Had to," Kollister said. "Telling you again now, you're to stay right here and keep out of it. I'm going after Vickers. If I don't make it, then it'll be up to you to —"

"You men — hold your fire!" The imperative command came from the lower end of the street. "I'm a U.S. Marshal. Throw down your guns!"

Matt Kollister had no need to look and determine the lawman's identity. It was time to cut and run for Mexico.

# 16

A lull settled over Shoham at Fred Larkin's shout. It was as if someone had closed a door somewhere, shutting off all sound, but the hush lasted for only a few moments. As abruptly as it had ceased, the shooting resumed, and once more the hot, dry air was filled with the crackle of guns and the smell of dust and burnt powder.

"They ain't paying that marshal no mind, Dave," one of the Diamond H riders said to the tall foreman. "You reckon we ought to pitch in and help him?"

Dave turned to Kollister. "You're the lawman, you reckon we ought?"

Matt stared off into the distance. Larkin would need help — plenty of it — but not the kind ordinary cowhands could give. Against Sam Vickers, Cherokee Smith and the like holed up along the street, he'd have small chance. And, if Larkin failed, then Shoham, too, would be lost. The outlaws, having already bested Hiram Huckaby's top guns, would take over and do as they pleased.

But to stay, to do what a small but strong voice deep within him was demanding, meant prison — a life where there was nothing but hate and bitterness and degrading cruelty. He could ignore that inner voice; he could simply shrug his shoulders and, after telling Dave and the Diamond H cowhands to do as they pleased, claim one of the loose horses standing off in the brush behind the feedstore. It was still a short ride to the border.

It would be easy, and Fred Larkin would never know he'd been in Shoham until he had crossed over the line and was well on his way to losing himself. Later, when things had quieted down, he could slip back over the border and pay a call on Seera Ford. Together they could decide what, if anything, lay in the future for them.

Could he do that? Could he ride off to safety and leave Shoham and the friends he'd made there to the mercies of Sam Vickers and his outlaws? Six, perhaps seven men were dead now — possibly more, as he had no way of knowing how the sentries he'd stationed on the roofs had fared. And, unless the shooting was brought to a halt, there'd be half a dozen more to bury before the day was over.

Matt rubbed at his jaw, glanced at Dave awaiting his reply. He had to choose, Kollister realized, and he had to do it now. Had he been anything but a lawman at heart, one dedicated to upholding right and opposing wrong, the choice could have been different. But, as such, Matt Kollister could follow only one course.

"The marshal's up against a stacked deck," he said, drawing his pistol and checking the cylinder to assure himself of its readiness. "He doesn't know what's going on, and he'll wade right in and get himself killed. I know him — I know how he figures — and the only men who'll throw down their guns like he wants are the wrong ones."

"For damn sure," Dave said. "Them outlaws ain't about to do that. You still aim to get on the other side of the street and go after Vickers and them?"

Matt slid his weapon back into its holster and nodded. "Need to borrow a horse. When I start across, you cover me from this side, tie up Vickers and his crowd long enough for me to make it."

Dave bobbed, signifying his understanding. "How about a couple of us going along to back you up?"

Kollister gave that only brief consideration. None of the men with the tall foreman looked to be other than what they were — ordinary ranch help with nothing more than average skill with weapons. They would pose more of a hindrance than a help, as he would find himself looking out for their welfare and thus be distracted from his purpose.

"Obliged, but you can favor me more by doing what I ask — scatter out along this side of the street and throw lead at those outlaws. That'll keep them busy not only while I'm crossing over, but after I'm there and start moving in."

"Sure," Dave said, and motioned to one of the riders. "Joe, get one of the horses for the marshal."

The cowhand moved away, trotting over to where they had left their mounts. Taking up the trailing reins of the nearest, a stocky, close-coupled little black, he quickly returned.

"Want to warn you again," Kollister said as he went into the saddle, "don't show yourself. Keep in between the buildings, or whatever else you can find to hide behind. You're dealing with killers. That shooting that's coming from on top of the buildings — those men are mine. Don't make a mistake and —"

"Hell, we know who's around here," Dave said. The hostility that he had displayed upon arrival had disappeared, and while there was no particular show of friendship now, all the Diamond H men were according him respect.

"Except you do," Matt said, rocking the saddle violently from side to side to be certain the cinch was tight. "String out now. I'll move down a ways and wait five minutes. That'll give you time to get set. When you open up, I'll make a run for it."

"Five minutes it is, Marshal," Dave said, and added, "Good luck."

"Same to you," Kollister responded. As the men hurried off, heading for the passageways between The Emporium, John Craig's place and Oren Yates's feedstore, he cut the black around and pointed him for Salem's Livery Barn, which was a considerable distance below that area along the street where the outlaws were making a stand. That fact, combined with the covering fire Dave and his men would give him, should make it possible to cross with small likelihood of being soon. Matt hoped luck would be with him and that it would work out that way; one of Vickers crowd spotting him could get in a shot as he broke into the open and end it all for him right there.

But Kollister was never a man to dwell on the dark probabilities, only upon the bright and positive. Usually, failure at such critical moments left a man dead anyway — in no condition to be aware of the fact.

Finally, Kollister reached the passageway alongside the Bullhead. There were no windows in that side of the building to reveal his presence, and he rode the black forward to the street, halting a yard or so short of the structure's corner. He could not see the area where the shooting was taking place, but the reports were fairly regular and he guessed the exchange was not about to slacken.

Across from him lay the Alamo Hotel; looking closely, he could see Seera standing in the adjoining restaurant. She was well back in the room, and that pleased him; not only was that a safety precaution, but she could not see him and would therefore be unaware of what he was about to do.

He'd head the black for the opening between the hotel and Wheeler's Meat Market, Matt decided. Studying the opposing row of buildings, he noted that there was a strong possibility that one of the outlaws would be hiding in the passageway separating the gun and saddle shop from the Trail's End Saloon. That could represent his greatest danger; a man in there would be certain to see him the instant he rode out into the street. Being near, he could also get in a quick shot. Matt reckoned he would have been better off attempting to cross farther down, but it was too late to change. Dave and the Diamond H riders would be opening up any moment, and he must take advantage of the distraction.

Anyway, he'd be ready if there was any sign of a man at the side of the gun shop. Drawing his pistol, he drew back the hammer; sliding as far as possible down the left side of his saddle, he waited.

A flurry of gunshots erupted at the far end of the street. Immediately, the firing on the part of the outlaws increased. Leaning well over the black like a trick rider, exposing as little of himself as possible, Matt slapped the horse sharply with the weapon he was holding and sent the animal plunging into the open.

All but out of the saddle, with the black's straining body shielding him, he threw his glance up the street. Huckaby lay behind the dead horse as he had left him and McEvee had not stirred. But there was one visible change: The sentry on the roof of The Emporium had been hit, and how hung head down over the edge. That brought a curse to the lawman's lips; he'd hoped to avoid death for any of the townsmen, but he guessed he should have known such would be impossible.

Movement next to the gun shop brought a halt to Matt's bitter thoughts and sent a warning surging through him. There was a man there as he'd feared. Matt saw him rise and bring up his arm to shoot. Kollister triggered the pistol in his hand. The bullet was wide, but close enough to turn the outlaw back, and by then it was too late. The black, running at top speed, had gained the side of the Alamo and the protection it afforded.

Righting himself on the heaving black, Kollister pulled the animal to a sliding halt and left the saddle in a long jump. If he was lucky, none of the outlaws except the one between Ferlin's and the Trail's End had seen his quick passage. It was important that the knowledge end there; the job of rooting out the Vickers gang would be much easier if they did not know that he was now behind them. To insure that, he must get to the outlaw before he could relay word to the others.

Running hard, Matt crossed the rear of the Alamo and the gun and saddle shop and turned into the passageway, pistol up and ready for instantaneous use. The outlaw, a stranger to him, spun at the sound of crunching sand and gravel; his eyes flared with surprise and fear, and he backed hastily and thoughtlessly into the street.

The man then realized his error and started to reverse himself. But a half dozen bullets, either from the men on the rooftops or those led by Huckaby's foreman, drove into the man and sent him sprawling into the dust.

Kollister spent no time there. Pivoting, he hurried back behind the buildings and trotted up to the Trail's End. He paused when he came abreast the saloon's door; there could be some of the outlaws inside. Simon Deal would not have welcomed them, but he would have been powerless to prevent their forcing their way into the building if they chose.

It was a long shot, and Kollister knew for certain there would be Vickers's men in and around the Palace and the structure housing the harbor shop and doctor's office. He'd have to let the Trail's End ride, drop back and go through it later after he'd accounted for the more definite positions.

Right then was when he could use a good, reliable partner, Matt thought. More careful now, he continued across the rear of the saloon for the narrow open space between it and the old hotel. It would have been good to know Fred Larkin was siding him; together they could have cleaned up Shoham's outlaw problem in short order.

But that hadn't been possible; Larkin would have insisted on following the law to its exact letter. First he would have taken Matt prisoner and jailed him, then assumed the chore of going after the outlaws on his own in defiance of the odds. That was the way Fred Larkin worked — strictly by the book.

Where was the old marshal, anyway? Had Larkin seen him crossing the street, hanging down on the side of the black like a sack of oats? Chances were he had. When the old lawman had called out his demand that the shooting stop, he had been somewhere at the lower end of the street — probably near the Bonanza. He would have probably gone there first for cover, once he realized he had run into the gun battle that was taking place.

Matt slowed; the corner of the saloon, beyond which lay the passageway, was a step ahead. Pistol up, he approached quietly. Pausing for a long breath at the mouth of its entrance, he then stepped quickly into its center.

Two men crouching at the opposite end whirled to face him — Calico Hays and a stranger. Kollister shook his head as they brought up their weapons to shoot.

"Don't —" he warned.

"The hell with you!" Hays shouted, and then staggered back as the lawman's bullet caught him in the chest.

The other outlaw fared little better. He dropped to one knee and fired hastily — too hastily. Matt's second shot smashed into him, sending him down into the accumulation of weeds and windblown trash that littered the floor of the passage.

Stepping up to the outlaw, Kollister collected the pistol the man had dropped and thrust it under his own belt. Apparently his bullet had not killed the man. Reloading his gun, he relieved Calico Hays of the weapon clutched in his stiffening fingers and threw it far back into the brush behind the saloon. Then, leveling his pistol at the wounded man, he smiled grimly.

"You want to lay here quiet while I go about my business, or you want me to put a bullet in your head to make sure? Makes no difference to me."

"I'm bad hit," the outlaw moaned.

"Then maybe you'd be better off dead like Calico," Matt suggested callously.

"No — no — I'll be all right!" the man replied hurriedly. "I — I won't try going nowhere!"

"Just keep remembering that," Kollister warned. "Show your face in the street and my men will blow your head off. I see you in the alley, I'll do the same."

"I ain't going nowhere — I'll be right here," the outlaw muttered. "I sure am bleeding bad."

"Stuff your bandanna in the hole," the lawman said, retracing his steps to the rear of the saloon.

The firing in the street had slacked off now to only an occasional shot, and there was the possibility, Matt realized, that the exchange between him and the two men in the passageway had been heard by some of the outlaws. The wall of the Palace, the next building in line, was only a stride away, and he was certain that several of Vickers's gang — and probably Sam himself — were inside.

He'd best not take on the old hotel yet; there was still that area on its far side to be cleared, as well as the barber shop and doctor's office. Once he had taken care of them, the time would be at hand to brace the men hiding inside the Palace.

Abruptly, the shooting along the street flared into a rapid exchange. Matt flinched

212

as a bullet splintered the board wall above him, reminding him that the passageway was a risky place in which to stand upright. Huckaby's hired hands, as well as the men on the rooftops, were laying down a blind fire in hopes of somehow hitting one of the well-concealed outlaws; generally they had no idea where their bullets might strike.

Crouched low now, Kollister crossed behind the Palace and halted at its rear corner. The faint breeze coming from the east was heavy with the smell of spent gunpowder, dust and — the lawman drew up sharply — tobacco smoke. Somewhere close-by a man was smoking.

Dropping to all fours, hat off, Matt eased forward. Sweat collected on his forehead and began to mist his eyes; pausing again, he brushed at it with the back of a hand.

"Maybe we ought to be pulling out of here," a voice said. "With Copio and a couple others leaving, and Buckshot getting hisself plugged, we ain't in such good shape no more."

"We're doing all right," came a reply. "There's still seven of us, and that's more'n enough."

Kollister tensed. It was Sam Vickers's voice. He mentioned seven men left — seven less three was the correct count. The odds were dropping in his favor.

"And there's that U.S. Marshal —"

"That old man? Hell, he ain't worth spit!"

"I ain't so dang sure. And what about that other jasper, the one we was talking to, the town's new marshal. He's got them cattlemen all lined up with him, along with the whole damned town!"

"Just take a look out there in the street and all you'll see's dead men. Them's your cattlemen. Only one still kicking is the old range bull himself, and he ain't going to last long. Far as them counter-jumpers up on the roofs go, they'll hop when I holler frog soon as they see how this is all coming out."

"Maybe, but you ain't said nothing about that new town marshal."

"I'll take care of him — personal," Vickers stated flatly. "Got a little squaring up to do with him. Now I want you to go find Calico and bring him here — he's with Ogilvie in there between —"

"I know where they are. What're you figuring to do?"

"Well, I reckon we've done enough shooting to make folks know we mean business. Aim for us to all go in the Palace and up to that front window. I'll sing out, tell these jaybirds they'd best forget bucking us and throw down their guns because we plain got them licked."

"They sure ought to be seeing that, with all them dead men laying in the street."

"Maybe, but just to make it sink in real good, I want Calico up there with his rifle. When I'm done talking, I'm going to let him pick off a couple of the counter-jumpers that are up there on the roof."

"Now, that'll sure make them believers!" the outlaw with Vickers declared. "I'll go fetch Calico."

"You do that — I'll be waiting inside," Vickers said.

Kollister drew back quickly. The door opening into the Palace was little more than an arm's length from him. Sam Vickers, to avoid any possibility of being hit by going to the front entrance, was certain to use it.

Taut, his own pistol in his right hand and the one taken from the man with Calico Hays in the left, Matt waited for the outlaws to round the corner.

# 17

Four left — Kollister recalled Sam Vickers' calculations. Seven he'd said, but he hadn't known about the man at Ferlin's Gun & Saddle Shop, or that Calico Hays and the outlaw called Ogilvie were out of it, too. Now, when Vickers and whoever it was with him were out of the picture, there would remain but two — one of whom was undoubtedly Cherokee Smith, probably the most dangerous member of the gang next to Vickers.

Kollister grinned wryly. *When Vickers and the man with him were out of the way!* He was putting blackberries in the pie before they were even picked! There was never anything sure in a confrontation when you went up against a man like Sam Vickers. Also, he had no idea who the outlaw with Sam might be — a hot-handed gunslinger, maybe. At such times everything was chance, and a man could only do his best.

"Be damn sure you tell Calico to bring his long gun when —"

Vickers, rounding the corner, cigar clamped between his teeth and a stranger at his side, broke off short. His hand streaked down for the gun at his side.

"How the hell —" he began, and fired from the hip.

But the outlaw triggered his weapon a full second too late. Kollister's bullet drilled into him dead center, slamming him into the man beside him. The stranger yelled as his own weapon was jolted from his grasp by Vickers's falling body. As he went to one knee, he threw up both hands.

"I quit!" he yelled frantically.

"Get on your feet!" the lawman snapped. The tension that had built within him was leveling off now that Vickers was taken care of. "And keep your hands up — high!"

The outlaw pulled himself upright, casting a quick glance at the lifeless shape of Sam Vickers laying in the dust, and faced Matt.

"What're you called?" Kollister asked curtly.

"Amos — Amos Green."

"All right, Green, I want to know who's inside the hotel — and whereabouts. Same goes for whoever's out there on the street."

Green wagged his head. He was a small man with thinning red hair, florid skin and darting black eyes. If he was an expert with a pistol, such had been nullified when Sam Vickers's body had crashed into him.

"I — I ain't sure —" he said falteringly.

"Think about it," Kollister cut in, raising his pistol. "After all the killing you and your bunch've done out there in the street, blowing your head off would be a pleasure."

"Well, there's Calico and Jed Ogilvie down by that saloon," Green said in a quick rush of words, "and next to the gun shop there's Billy Vee, and —"

"They're out of it," the lawman interrupted in a harsh voice. "Who else?"

Green hesitated, a frown creasing his face. There was no shooting in the street; it was filled at the moment with only a tight hush and the ever-lingering odor of burnt powder and dust.

"That mean they're dead?"

Kollister nodded briskly. "Two for sure. Expect the third one's done by now. What about the hotel?"

"Cherokee's in there, and you sure ain't going to sneak up on him! He's got Indian blood —"

"Who else?"

"Ben Wilson," Green replied; when the

lawman pressed the question with his cold eyes, he added, "Hell, Marshal, they're all that's left! You done killed off everybody."

"Expect that about evens it up for the men you shot down."

"Now, that was Sam's idea!" Green protested. "Don't go blaming me for —"

"You can tell the judge that when he sentences you to swing for what you've done," Matt said. Reaching out, he grasped the outlaw by the shoulder and whirled him about.

"Move," he ordered. "We're going in the back door of the Palace, and you'll be walking in front of me. Want you to take me straight to where Cherokee and Wilson are. My gun will be against your backbone all the way, so if you make one wrong turn, I'll blow you in two. Understand?"

Green mumbled a reply and nodded. Arms still up, he started for the rear door of the old hotel.

"Put your hands down," the lawman directed, keeping his voice low.

The outlaw dropped his arms and, walking carefully, stepped up to the heavy panel. Hesitating briefly, he grasped the knob and turned it, pushing the door inward as he entered. Kollister, good as his threat, was close behind with the hard muzzles of his forty-five digging into the man's spine.

The hall they were in was narrow and dark, the only light coming from somewhere ahead. Pushing the door shut behind him, Matt nudged Green with the gun barrel and they continued. A voice could be heard from off to their right, but he doubted it would be either of the two outlaws; they would be in the front of the building, at a window where they could shoot.

A shadow crossed the hallway ahead of Kollister and his prisoner. Immediately Green threw himself to one side.

"Look out!" he yelled. "It's the law!"

Kollister dropped to the floor as the shadow spun. It was Cherokee Smith. Matt fired as the deerskin-clad outlaw whipped out his weapon. The bullet was low; it caught Smith in the hip, wheeled him around, and drove him solidly against the wall where he hung momentarily and then slowly settled on his side. Cherokee the Deadly had been no problem at all.

The lawman came to his feet quickly. Rushing forward, he clubbed the cowering Amos Green in the head with his pistol, stunning him into immobility. Kicking Smith's weapon aside, he gained the end of the hall where Cherokee had appeared; his partner would be close-by.

The corridor led on to a room at the front of the hotel that served as a lobby. Matt could see only a part of the area from where he stood, and there was no one in evidence.

"Wilson!" he called sharply. "I want you to throw down your gun and walk out to where I can see you — with your hands up!"

There was no response. The only sound in the stuffy, heat-filled building was the raspy breathing of Amos Green.

"I know you're in there, and if I have to come after you, I'll kill you same as I had to do Vickers."

Another silence followed; then a deep, hoarse voice said, "Sam's dead?"

"He is — along with Calico and Ogilvie and a couple others. And I've got Cherokee and Amos Green laying here on the floor. You're the last one, Wilson — what's it going to be?"

Again there was only a stillness. It was broken finally when a pistol thumped onto the center of the dusty old lobby floor. Kollister, alert for any trick, remained tight against the wall, weapon ready. Shortly, a squat, slope-shouldered man stepped into view, arms above his head as he'd been told to do.

A sigh escaped the lawman's lips. That ended it, and it had been easier than he'd expected. Moving up to Wilson, he pushed the outlaw roughly toward the hotel's front door. Instantly the man drew back.

"I can't go out there! They'll fill me plumb full of lead soon as I show my face!"

"It's a chance you're going to take," Kollister replied indifferently. Keeping Wilson in front of him, he opened the door and stepped out onto the small porch.

"Hold your fire — I'm the marshal!" he shouted. "It's all over!"

There had been a brief moment of stunned relief when Matt Kollister appeared with the outlaw shielding him and made his announcement. Then a cheer had broken out from the ranch hands on the opposite side of the street that was quickly taken up by the men on the roofs and the townspeople close enough to hear.

The area between the rows of buildings had filled quickly. Men rushed up to congratulate Kollister and relieve him of his prisoner; others hurried off to take possession of the other outlaws, both dead and wounded.

Through it all, Matt's response was automatic, wooden. His attention was centered on Seera Ford standing off to one side waiting for the crush of admirers to spend itself

— and on the slight figure with the star of a Deputy U.S. Marshal facing him from across the way. He'd won — and he'd lost, Kollister thought. Moving forward with Craig, Yates, Salem and the rest of the town's Council, with a large number of local citizens trailing him, he crossed to where the lawman stood.

"Morning, Fred," he said, nodding.

The marshal's head moved slightly. "Morning, Matthew. I'm a mite surprised to find you here wearing a badge. Was figuring you'd be on the other side of the Mexican border by now."

"He could've been, had he wanted," Tom Salem said quickly, recognizing the federal lawman and his purpose for being in Shoham. "Stayed here to help us."

"We had us an outlaw problem — along with a bit of trouble with the ranchers," Craig added.

"Was more like a war," Larkin observed dryly, and favored Kollister with a quick, thin-lipped smile. "Can see you ain't lost your touch. Still a mite too quick with that six-shooter you're carrying — but I reckon you done what you had to."

Matt shrugged, turned his eyes to Seera. She was walking toward him through the crowd swarming in the street. She had realized who Larkin was, and a worried look had now replaced her usually serene features.

"You willing to move out?" Larkin asked. "Plenty of daylight left."

"He ain't going nowhere with you, Marshal," Hank Beatty stated quietly before Matt could answer. "He belongs to us, and we ain't letting you take him no place."

"Specially back to serve time for that raw deal he got!" It was Levi Marcus. His voice was firm and decisive, and in no way reflected the shy, meek man he was considered to be.

Larkin shook his head. "Now, don't you folks go flying off the handle and do something you'll be real sorry for. Did I have the say-so, Matthew Kollister could go free right now — I've never known a better lawman. But he's been tried and convicted and sentenced, and he'll be the first to tell you that the law has to be upheld."

"Not when the judge and the jury railroaded him to cover up for some highfalutin muckety-muck!"

"Could be true — I never was one to believe he'd do anything that wasn't according to the oath he swore, but it just ain't up to me to do any judging."

"Well, maybe it is for us," John Craig said.

"We're a sort of country to ourselves down here, nobody wanting us. Makes us sort of look after ourselves. Now, I want you to understand how it is: It'll be no big problem to keep you busy while we see that Kollister gets across the border, or —"

"Or what?" Larkin pressed coolly.

"Or you can leave him here and let him keep on being our town marshal while we get that murder charge they trumped up looked into."

The lawman frowned, drew a blue bandanna from his hip pocket and mopped at his face and neck. "I ain't sure you can do that — open up a trial."

"We can try," Craig replied. "We've got some pretty big men around here — Hiram Huckaby for one — who'll lag for him, and Hiram ain't one to spare the horses when he goes after something. He's been shot up some in this little fracas we had, but the doc says he'll be all right."

"And there ain't a man, woman or child in this town that won't stand by the Marshal," Salem declared. "Can bet your last dollar on that."

Larkin carefully folded the bandanna and thrust it back into a pocket. He shifted his attention to Kollister, who was standing with an arm around Seera. A hush had

225

fallen over the crowd as they awaited the government man's words.

"I'm going to leave it up to you, Matthew," he said. "I'm willing to let things ride so's these friends of yours can talk to the governor, and I —"

"Like Craig said, we don't belong to New Mexico *or* Texas," someone in the crowd reminded the lawman. "There ain't nothing they —"

"It's the governor of Colorado you'll have to square with," Larkin snapped, frowning at the interruption. "What I was going to say is, if you're willing to give me your word that you'll stay right here till we get an answer, and not go skipping across the border if things don't work out right, I'll string along with the idea."

Kollister smiled and extended an arm. "Here's my hand, Marshal — and you've got my word."

The older man accepted the assurance with a firm clasp and a nod of his head. "From you that's all I need," he said, and began to shoulder his way through the crowd toward his horse, somewhere down beyond the Bullhead Saloon. "You'll be hearing from me."

"I'll be here," Matt replied.

# ABOUT THE AUTHOR

**Ray Hogan** was born in Missouri but has spent most of his life in New Mexico. His father was an early Western marshal and lawman, and Hogan himself has spent a lifetime researching the West. He has written over 100 books, including *Outlaw's Pledge, Pilgrim, The Hell Raiser, The Doomsday Trail, Decision at Doubtful Canyon,* and 24 titles in the bestselling Shawn Starbuck series, all available in Signet paperback. His work has been filmed, televised, and translated into sixteen languages.

We hope you have enjoyed this Large Print book. Other Thorndike, Wheeler, and Chivers Press Large Print books are available at your library or directly from the publishers.

For information about current and upcoming titles, please call or write, without obligation, to:

Publisher
Thorndike Press
295 Kennedy Memorial Drive
Waterville, ME 04901
Tel. (800) 223-1244

or visit our Web site at:

www.gale.com/thorndike
www.gale.com/wheeler

OR

Chivers Large Print
published by BBC Audiobooks Ltd
St James House, The Square
Lower Bristol Road
Bath BA2 3SB
England
Tel. +44(0) 800 136919
email: bbcaudiobooks@bbc.co.uk
www.bbcaudiobooks.co.uk

All our Large Print titles are designed for easy reading, and all our books are made to last.